THE FLOW

CAROLINE MARTIN

LOVELL PRESS

For Sam and Alice

LONDON HERALD
MAY 4TH, 2009

Second bank collapse causes chain reaction

Late last night, the Bank of England gave up its attempts to find a white knight to rescue the ailing Royal Welsh Bank. Stock markets plummeted across the globe in response a[s] the UK government was forced to issue a statement in which they pledged to stand behind the pound. But market analysts fear that currency speculation will drive down its value when the markets open today.

LONDON HERALD
JULY 5TH, 2009

Warrant issued for arrest of top treasury officials

Metropolitan Police have confirmed that they are now hunting for several individuals in connection with what has been called the 'biggest fraud in the history of Britain'. The unnamed officials are thought to have conspired with the three missing government ministers to artificially fix interest rates and thereby defraud the government of millions of pounds. The Prime Minister is being recalled to Buckingham Palace today.

LONDON HERALD
JULY 6TH, 2009

'You are not fit to govern,' says Queen.

In a historic meeting at Buckingham Palace, the Queen has used an ancient act of Parliament to remove the Prime Minister from his post and called an immediate general election. She has appointed a senior member of her Royal Advisory Panel to act as an interim head of government. In a TV interview scheduled for this afternoon, she is expected to announce that elections will be held in three months time. In the meantime, the Army has been put on high alert and a state of emergency has been declared across the country.

LONDON HERALD
AUGUST 19TH 2009

Riots spread to all major towns

The Army used tear gas and plastic bullets last night in a tenth night of disturbance across Britain.

With the Prime Minister having fled and continued questions being asked about his involvement in the financial scandals of the past few months, the ordinary citizens of Britain are expressing their outrage in an increasingly physical manner. Neither the Army nor the police force is large enough to cope with this mass public rebellion. With twenty-five murders last night, it is only a matter of time before they will be forced to use live rounds.

LONDON HERALD
SEPTEMBER 26TH 2009

New political movement gathers momentum

You may not have heard about them until very recently, but The Optimas Party have actually been operating here in the UK for several years. Before the Collapse, they had been quietly fielding candidates in local elections. But now they have stepped things up a gear and are making a bid for the national stage.

In every by-election, one of their candidates will stand. And most polls show that their brand of faith based politics is appealing to more and more voters as the security situation becomes worse across the UK.

LONDON HERALD
OCTOBER 5TH 2009

Salvation?

Across the country, voters came out in force yesterday in support of religious 'prophet' Nathaniel Jefferies and his political followers in The Optimas Party.

Across the Atlantic, his ultra conservative religion has been dubbed a cult.

Questions have been asked about the methods used to obtain conformance in the enormous communities in which his followers live. But what will it mean for Britain, still reeling from the shock of the Collapse? His places of worship, known as Sacellums, are being constructed across the country. And now The Optimas Party has swept to power in Westminster.

Chapter One

THE FLOW

Eight years later...

I'm getting impatient. I skim my hand across the screen of the thin metal tablet and call up the keyboard - again. I type the name of the city that I'm researching into the Flow search box - for the second time in less than a minute. The screen blackens and, finally, a list of links appears; the tourist office for the Northern Territories, the Australian Embassy and several holiday firms offering trips exploring the Outback.

But in the instant before the list materialises, I catch a glimpse of the picture again. The one that appeared a few seconds ago - when my screen shut itself down.

Was it an old photograph? It seemed to be the head and shoulders of a man, dressed sombrely. He had a huge white beard. But I don't recognise him at all.

'Alexa,' my mother calls from downstairs. 'It's time to go. We can't be late for prayers.'

'I know. I'm coming,' I shout back.

But before I go down, I can't resist checking my messages quickly, so I swipe my forefinger across the glass and explode my homepage on the tablet screen. An array of icons is flashing information at me; a couple of messages from school friends, a Flow clip of a skateboarding cat, and a coupon for a free milkshake at my favourite coffee shop. Just as I'm about to close it down, a reminder pops up about the Screening tonight. It sounds like a good one: a film about a new band, The Chills, and their tour of the New World. Looking at the essay half written on my desk, I make a quick assessment; if I race back from the Sacellum later, I reckon I might finish it in time to go.

'Alexa!'

'The system is playing up again mum,' I tell her as I sprint downstairs into the front hall, taking the narrow steps two at a time and nearly tripping up on the last few.

We grab our robes from the hooks by the front door. I push my head through the small hole in the middle of the sheet of fabric and let the long folds of white silk cascade down over my shoulders. Then I tighten the elastic around my throat a little and pull the hood up tightly over my short blonde hair. Before my mother opens the door we check one another.

'Tighter Alexa; I can still see your neck. Am I OK?'

'Fine mum. Stop worrying,' I reply, but I'm not really looking because she's always immaculate.

'It's important sweetheart. We mustn't use our appearance to stand out...'

'Whatever mum. Come on; let's just go, can't we? I want to get back and finish this assignment. I wouldn't mind watching the film tonight. Everyone at school will be talking about it tomorrow.'

I rush through the front door and leave my mother to lock up the house. Out in the street, there are people everywhere, all dressed in their variously coloured robes, marching towards the Sacellum. There is a warm buzz of chatter in the air with neighbours greeting each other enthusiastically, children playing and everyone preparing to celebrate the end of another working day. For a few seconds, I stop and watch them all. The group of boys kicking a football down the middle of the street. The old couple who live opposite us, walking hand in hand on the pavement, watching the boys and clearly reminiscing about their own distant youth. The gaggle of young mothers gathered in a huddle, carrying babies on their hips and chattering about sleepless nights.

It is a twice-daily ritual for us all to make this journey to our place of worship and when I was younger, the evening visit was possibly my favourite hour of the day. I used to find the early morning prayers too tiring. But at the end of the day, being able to see everyone I knew and loved had always seemed like a treat not a chore. As an only child, the community at the Sacellum gave me people to play with. With no relatives nearby, the old people in the services had become as good as grandparents to me.

Watching them all now, I feel the pull of this 'family' for a few seconds. But then, I am overwhelmed by a newer – different - feeling. When my mother's friend, Jenny Baker, raises her arm to wave us over to her side of the street, all I feel is a sense of dread and claustrophobia. I would so much rather be on my own. I have to walk with my mother, but I really don't want to listen to Mrs. Baker as well this evening. So I look away and pretend I haven't seen her.

'What were you saying about the system?' my mother asks me when she reaches me. 'I don't have enough money to buy you a new tablet.'

'I know. It wasn't the tablet,' I say, setting off quickly towards the Sacellum before my mother has chance to spot Mrs. Baker. 'That guy down the road seems to have fixed whatever was wrong with it last week. This was the Flow. It's being interrupted. When I searched, I got a picture on the screen and it made the tablet crash.'

'I'm sure the Party will fix that,' my mother replies as she checks her robes again and smoothes them with the palms of her hands. *Time is money* as they say. They can't have the Flow slow down or the quantum trading in the banks will be affected. Real time prices will be lost and trading opportunities will be missed.'

I stare at her, speechless. I can't imagine what she

knows about real time prices. And if she knows anything about them at all, then I really don't know why she is here - walking along this suburban street, one of the classified masses going to the Sacellum. She drives me crazy with her obsession with the rules and regulations of our lives, her unquestioning obedience to the Party. She smiles and waves to our neighbours, repeating the choreographed set of actions that will absolve us of our sins. And she doesn't stand out at all.

But then she goes and says something like that; as if she actually understands all the technical jargon that we see on the TV or the Flow. And I'm left wondering if I know anything about her at all. I've tried asking her about her life, what she did when I was young, and she just says she was a sinner. She won't tell me what her crime was, or her punishment. But the look of fear in her eyes tells me that it is a subject, like that of my father's whereabouts, that she will never, ever, discuss with me.

For a moment or two, I can see the curiosity about the Flow in her eyes and I notice that she is absent-mindedly twisting the bracelet hidden beneath her elasticated sleeve. But then it is gone; replaced by her everyday expression of passive devotion and acceptance.

When we arrive at the Sacellum, we enter the small wooden porch. We rearrange ourselves into single file and begin to utter our requests for forgiveness as we pass the image of our prophet, Nathaniel Jefferies. Then we make our way into the vast interior and at this point I am separated from my mother; sent to join my equivalents in the central atrium whilst she moves to the back with the other divorcees in purple.

As she leaves me, I think about the bracelet - her one truly beautiful possession. It has two simple strands of gold twisted around one another with thin strands of silver like the rungs of a ladder between them. The Sacellum has decreed that such ostentatious items are never to be displayed. But she never removes it; she just hides it. And she has told me so many stories about where it came from that I have no idea of the truth. I have however noticed that her hands are drawn to it whenever she is deep in thought.

My own Sacellum-sanctioned versions, a bundle of ragged, thread, Significance Bracelets, are just visible at my wrists. Each one was given to me by a friend on an important occasion. There's certainly no way that they can be considered beautiful but each one does have meaning I suppose.

'Good evening,' comes the Pastor's voice from over the loudspeaker. 'Quickly into your places please.'

I always like the sight of the Sacellum when it's full... it's a bit like a giant paint box. Each section of the building is filled with hundreds of people wearing matching robes, separated from other groups by ropes or wooden barriers. As I queue slowly to reach my designated place, I watch the pre-schoolers fidgeting over to my right, all dressed in dark blue. Some older children in light blue always sit behind them with strict instructions to keep them under control. Seeing them, I have a sudden flashback to a sharp kick in the bottom from a young boy who had regularly sat behind me with the same task.

A shove from a Sacellum worker in black stops my daydreaming and I'm steered towards the middle of the Sacellum, to the other girls currently being evaluated: all in our white cloaks.

'Here... Lexi,' comes an urgent voice from my right.

'Tish! Is there room for me?' I ask the statuesque girl who has called my name. I try to squeeze past three older girls who have stopped in front of me and are getting ready to pray.

'Yes – come on. Hey, let her past you three,' Laetitia says in her bossiest voice and although they turn around to argue, all three girls stop short when they see who has spoken.

Silently they move their cushions and I walk to stand next to my oldest friend.

'Do you think it will be quick tonight?' I ask her, hoping for some inside knowledge. 'I need to get back and finish that essay so that I can go to the Screen later. You coming?'

'Hmm. No, I don't think I'm going to be able to.'

'But you never miss... '

The Sacellum whistle blasts and I bow my head. Suddenly I feel Tish's small warm hand reaching for mine and I give it a squeeze. I turn to look at her downcast face and I see tears in her eyes.

'Tish?' I whisper but she just shakes her head as the Pastor begins to speak.

For twenty minutes, we recite the standard prayers and requisite answers. And all the time, as I hold tightly to her hand, I can feel Tish trembling beside me. It's really unnerving me - it is so unlike her.

And then the Pastor stops.

Apprehensively, I look up at him and see that he is gazing over towards us; the two groups of young people dressed in white – boys on the left of the aisle and we girls on the right.

'This afternoon we held a special meeting of the Quorum,' he begins.

I turn to Tish and watch a tear tumble down her flushed cheek as she stares at her feet. Why won't she look at me?

'You will be delighted to hear that we have successfully managed to allocate two of our young people who were under evaluation,' continues the Pastor.

I hear excited gasps from the paired couples in the main body of the Sacellum standing together, dressed in gold. At the same time, the widowed old people in silver, on the seats at the front, turn and smile at us benevolently.

I look from the Pastor to Tish and back again and feel my mouth go dry, whilst my palms begin to sweat. All the air seems to have disappeared from the room.

'No... no, please let it not be me. Please let it not be me,' I say over and over again in my head and as I say it, I imagine my mother's face, at the back. I'm not ready for this.

Chapter Two

THE ALLOCATION

The Pastor continues to speak and I am shaking as much as Tish now.

'My friends... As a signal to you of his complete and utter devotion to the Creator... I can now announce... that Felix Canter, our respected and revered Optimas Party leader here in Oxford... has decided... '

And then he pauses for what seems like an age.

Come on, I think, *what has he decided? Just tell me.*

'That he will relinquish his beautiful daughter, Laetitia, in her first year of evaluation,' he finally proclaims.

What? What did he just say?

I stare at the Pastor and then down at the long brown

fingers interlaced with my own.

Whilst the surprise ripples around the assembled community, I lift my head to gaze at her face. Finally, she is now looking at me; her mouth quivering, shoulders slumped and her usual composure in a crumpled heap at her feet.

'Why? Why not let you wait the usual three or four years?' I ask in a harsh whisper.

'I don't know,' she mumbles, sounding confused and fearful. 'He just told me before we set off to come here.'

'He has agreed that she will be paired with the son of our most successful local businessman, Jan Svoboda,' the Pastor continues flamboyantly. 'Lukas, please will you come up to the Altar.'

'Lukas Svoboda?' I say to Tish.

A tall, slim figure makes his way to the aisle from the centre of the group of boys in white. He begins to walk towards the grinning Pastor. He looks as terrified at Tish.

'Dad wouldn't tell me who it was. Just said it was a fantastic match and he couldn't turn it down.'

'But you're too young Tish. Fourteen is too young... '

As I speak, we hear her name and know she must go to join Lukas on the steps of the Altar. We have seen too many times what happens if you delay and Tish starts to move towards the aisle. I walk with her, holding onto her hand for as long as possible. My heart feels as if it is being torn in two as she is grabbed by the outstretched arms of the golden clad couples lining the aisle. I want to shout at them all to stop. Beg them not to send her to a future with a boy she barely knows. But I can't.

In a daze I listen whilst the Pastor introduces them to

one another and presents them with their new robes. They are supposed to mark the wearer out as a celebrity until their wedding on the sixteenth birthday of the older of the two. But as the red silk floats down over Tish's white shroud, it just looks like a bloody stain to me; a mark of oppression and perhaps even violence.

Lukas Svoboda. What do I know of him? Not much. I believe his family were Czech originally, but they've lived here since one of the Great Wars I think. I vaguely remember my mother once talking about the factory that his father runs; telling me that it was considered a good place to work. I've heard that his father gave it over to the Party willingly so I'm pretty sure the whole family are very devout; they are certainly always at the Sacellum. That must be why Felix Canter liked the match so much.

Scanning the couples in front of me, I have no difficulty in spotting Lukas' mother and father now; beaming as they are congratulated by everyone around them. Tish's mother and father are moving through the crowd and are nearly alongside the Svobodas. Although Felix Canter is holding out his hand and grinning like a fool, Tish's mother looks less sure. Trailing her larger than life husband, she appears rather sheepish as she is bombarded with enthusiastic declarations of approval.

And Lukas himself? I certainly don't know anything about him because we are kept separate at school. But I think he is in the same year as us. So hopefully that gives Tish some time before the wedding. I don't think I've ever seen him at a Screening though. I hope he's not one of those boys who spend all day in front of the Flow when he's not praying. Tish doesn't deserve that.

The whistle blasts again. We are instructed to leave and the Pastor swivels Tish and Lukas around to face us all. As I wait in line to file out of the Sacellum past them, I watch them both shaking the outstretched hands of the congregation. I have to admit that Tish now seems to be doing a fantastic job of pretending to be delighted. I suppose she's watched her father often enough to know how to deal with a crowd of supporters.

But as her oldest friend I can see the signs of her unhappiness like flashing neon lights over her head. She has a slightly wild look in her eyes and her smile is excruciatingly fixed on her face. I know I am watching the biggest performance of her life.

I look at Lukas, standing awkwardly alongside her. His every movement appears painfully self-conscious. One of my neighbours, Mrs Novak, reaches to embrace him, and his face turns the colour of a tomato. Once I am level with him, I can see that his hands are shaking; he is almost rigid with fear. And he looks completely out of his depth alongside Tish.

'I'll come and see you tomorrow,' I whisper to Tish as we embrace. 'I'm so sorry.'

The line moves and we are forced apart once more. This suddenly feels like the end of my childhood as well as her own. I don't understand how it can be the right way to live, with old men in a committee deciding which person you should spend the rest of your life with.

But even as these doubts rise up in my mind, I realise

that they are dangerous. I check the fellow members of the community. No, they are so absorbed with this exciting development that they are oblivious to me.

Outside, I look for my mother. After the events of the service, she will want me to walk home with her. Despite what she will say, I know she'll be pretty shaken up by the announcement. It will have reminded her that it could be me soon.

Scanning the crowds to look for her, I see a face staring directly at me. It is the man who lives four doors along from us. The one who fixed my tablet. There is no doubt about it; he is looking very particularly at me, and he raises his hand to make a tiny acknowledgment of that fact. His face is very serious and I notice that he is wearing a white sash across his black robes to indicate that he has devoted his life to serving the community and has opted never to be paired. Having only encountered him as a fixer of tablets, I am surprised to see he is so devout.

I feel a stab of panic that he might know exactly what I was just thinking.

Chapter Three

THE MESSAGE

'It's for the best,' my mother says as we set off for home.

'How can you say that?'

'It's what we need now. We need people to make rational choices that will ensure the country doesn't fall apart again. We need sensible unions and families who will draw together and make us stronger.'

'You sound just like the Pastor.'

'And what exactly is wrong with that?'

I look at her earnest face.

'Oh nothing... but it all sounds so...'

'Yes?'

'So... sensible - and you know it.'

'I'll tell you what I know Alexa. I know that life became unbearable before. When people just did what they wanted and no one cared for their community or planned for the future.'

'And how will Tish marrying Lukas Svoboda prevent that happening again?'

'You know the answer to that. They have been carefully assessed for suitability.'

'What do old men know?'

'They both come from strong families,' she says, ignoring me. 'Who will support them as they get to know one another. Then together, Lukas and Tish will bring up their children to respect the Creator and the world he has given us.'

'She could find someone herself that would do all that - when she's ready.'

'Maybe... but history tells us that too many people value the wrong things when they make these choices.'

'You and dad didn't - did you?'

My mother stops walking and looks at me. She doesn't answer, so I change tack.

'But what if it had been me mum?'

She starts to walk again.

'But it wasn't.'

'But next time it might be.'

'No, it will be many months, if not years, before you are allocated. You forget that Tish is a special case.'

'And you forget she's my friend.'

She pauses.

'I do *not* forget that. I promise you,' she says, more quietly.

'Then how can you defend them?'

'I'm not defending them,' she says, sounding anxious now. 'But you mustn't talk like this Lexi.'

'I'm not allowed to question anything?'

'No, it's too dangerous.'

'What do you mean?'

'Nothing. You just ... don't understand the implications of what you say.'

'Don't I?'

'Lexi please,' she continues. 'Trust me. I'm merely pointing out that sometimes people do not make good choices... and too many bad choices can have unexpected consequences. We need political, economic and spiritual stability in this country.'

'I still don't see why that has to mean pairings when you are sixteen.'

'Family is everything to the Sacellum, you know that. Families will hold society together and provide for one another and for those of us who are... alone.'

I can't think what to say to this. I know what we have always been taught at school and in the Sacellum; the stories of what happened before. But I also know that my mother *would* have been devastated if it had been me and I wish she would admit it. It's not as if I'm going to report her. There have been some terrible denunciations of parents by their children in the past few years, but I wouldn't ever do that.

'I'm going to finish that assignment,' I say, as soon as we are home. I yank off my cloak and throw it vaguely in the direction of the peg on the back of the door. I hear my mother sigh sadly and watch her as she bends to

16

pick up the discarded pile of fabric, shake it and put it back in its rightful place.

Once in my room, I shut the door and lie down on my bed. I stare at the posters above me, stuck to the ceiling with peeling, yellowing tape. They show my favourite band, Xentricity. I reach across to my bedside table and feel for the 'play' button on my music player. Closing my eyes, I let the pulsing music flood over me.

I concentrate on the lead singer's soothing voice and the familiar lyrics. After a couple of tracks, I begin to feel slightly happier, more confident that Tish will be OK. It occurs to me that the couples in the Sacellum always seem happy enough and Lukas might not be so bad. Perhaps I shouldn't be so pessimistic.

I think about him again, remembering him standing next to Tish on the Sacellum steps...

'Lexi!' comes my mother's voice from downstairs.

Irritated, I put my head over the stair banister to shout down to her. But before I can utter a word, I find myself looking directly into the very face that had just appeared in my imagination.

'Lukas? Oh... er - how can I help?'

'Alexa, I am not sure that this boy should be here in our house this late,' interjects my mother.

'Mum, I know OK, but it's only seven. It's not as if it's after curfew,' I say, walking down the stairs.

'I won't be here long Mrs. Drachmann,' Lukas adds.

'Can you get us some drinks mum?' I ask and start off towards the front room. 'I'll talk to Lukas in here.'

'I guess so,' she mutters.

'Thank you Mrs. Drachmann,' Lukas adds. 'I just want a moment with Alexa. I'll be gone long before the lights come on.'

Lukas follows me along the hallway. We rarely have guests and when I open the sitting room door, I panic slightly. The two of us are required to sit at least three feet apart and our only two seats, an armchair and a small sofa, are currently side by side so that my mother and I can both watch television. Quickly, I sweep a pile of magazines to one end of the small sofa, brush the cat hair off the armchair, and drag it towards the TV, away from the sofa a little.

'Why don't you sit there?' I say to Lukas, pointing at the armchair.

'Thanks.'

'Is everything OK?'

'Yes,' he begins and then pauses while I just stare at him.

'I'll look after her you know,' he blurts out eventually. He is looking at me with such a desperate expression that I almost laugh. 'Laetitia I mean. I know that you and she are friends; I've seen you together. I just thought that I should come and see you to tell you that.'

'You didn't need to.'

I hear a harshness in my own voice that surprises me.

'No, but it's what I wanted to do. I will tell Laetitia too... but she might believe it if she also hears it from you.'

I think about this for a while, wondering if Lukas is being thoughtful or manipulative.

'I'm sure you'll try to take care of her.'

I would love to ask him how a boy can look after a wife, but I am accustomed to the need for caution.

'Did you know about it? The allocation?' I ask instead.

'No, nothing. I was out this afternoon, and I didn't see my parents. I've suspected that my father would want me to be allocated quite quickly though. He and my mother married when they were pretty young.'

'How old are you then?'

'Just fifteen... so at least there'll be some time before the ceremony.'

'Hmm. I guess so.'

But as I remember some of the plans that Tish and I had been making for the summer holidays, I feel a building resentment towards the person for whom they will all now be abandoned.

'You can still see her you know. I mean... once we are together,' Lukas is saying when my attention returns to him. 'I wouldn't take Laetitia away from her friends.'

He says this, but I know that our lives of listening to music, painting our nails and chatting about videos we've watched on the Flow are now basically over. No matter how kind and understanding Lukas may prove to be, he and Tish will be living the life of a paired couple and I will have lost her forever; my friend will be living with this boy that she has never spoken to before.

'I don't know what to say to you Lukas. About Tish, I mean.'

'I know.'

'I just don't really know how I can help... what you want.'

'Nothing; it's not like that,' he says defensively. 'I just wanted to...'

'What?'

'Oh I don't know. It's all still too much for me to get my head around. I thought perhaps...'

'Yes?'

'Perhaps you could tell me a little about her.'

I stare at him. And then the penny drops; he is as confused by events as Tish and I are.

'I'd be really grateful if you could tell me anything that will make things a bit easier when I meet her.'

About an hour later, having interrupted us twice on spurious errands, my mother has finally had enough.

'OK, it's time you were going now I'm afraid Lukas. It is nearly eight and I'm sure your parents will be wondering where you've got to.'

'Yes, sorry. Thank you for letting me come in Mrs. Drachmann. I'm grateful for your hospitality,' Lukas replies and rises to follow my mother out of the room.

'Sorry I kept you. Perhaps you had meant to go to the Screen tonight?' I find myself asking.

'No, it's no problem. I don't actually go to the Screenings. I find them... difficult.'

There is no time to ask him what he means by this; my mother whisks him out of the front door, shutting it hastily in the middle of my goodbye.

'Mum! Did you have to be so rude?'

'Sorry, but he was here too long sweetheart. It's not proper.'

Shaking my head at her oversensitivity to our rules

and regulations, I almost remind her that he has just been promised to my best friend. But I can't be bothered.

On my desk is my half completed schoolwork and I sit down in front of my tablet to finish it off. But before I start, I automatically check my homepage; a new message has appeared in my mail account. The subject box is blank so I open the text. There is just one sentence.

'We thought you might be interested in joining us.'

I look up at the sender details and don't see a name that I recognise. I should delete it immediately. I'm not sure how it has got through our household security software but I know the protocol is to just put it in the trash. And yet I don't.

A ping, and a second message arrives in the inbox.

'If you wish to join us then click here.'

This time there is a link for me to connect to. I think about all the warnings we have been given in Flow safety seminars at school - about some outcasts who call themselves Scientia. My mother says they are people who have refused to allow the Creator into their lives. She says they are dangerous. She seems perpetually worried that they'll try to contact me. And now, for the first time in my life, I wonder if she was right to be concerned. If I click on the link, perhaps there will be spotlights over our house and the two of us will be taken away by the Task Force.

I hesitate and then hear a third ping.

'We saw you in the Sacellum this evening... You are

right to be concerned about what is going on.'

The spasm of pure fear that clenches my stomach is like nothing I have ever known. I slam down the lid of the tablet.

But after a moment, I open it back up again... and press delete, three times in quick succession.

And then I stare at the screen, waiting to see what happens next.

Chapter Four

THE REQUEST

I'm tired. I sat staring at my tablet for an hour last night, but no more messages arrived.

Even so, with Tish's allocation and Lukas' visit to contemplate as well, I barely slept. Now, watching the shafts of sunlight explode around the edges of the curtains, I realise that I may as well give up any hope of getting more rest. So I pull on some comfortable clothes and I'm about to go downstairs for some breakfast when I hear the doorbell ring. I look at the clock: seven a.m.

I listen for my mother's voice, but the only sound is a second, longer bell ring. Opening my bedroom door, I hear that she is still in the shower and the bell just keeps ringing.

A minute later, I'm sliding the chain across and opening the front door. On the doorstep is a man, dressed in black robes with a white sash across his chest. He motions for me to come outside.

'Alexa Drachmann?'

'Yes.'

'I think you need to come with me please.'

It is the man from the Sacellum; the one who fixed my tablet. As I listen to him, all I can think about are the messages in my trash folder and the stories I have heard about the way people are treated who question the Party and the Sacellum.

Suddenly, I feel my mother's presence behind me.

'Brother Benedict, how good to see you. Is everything alright?' she asks nervously.

At first I'm surprised that she knows his name. Until I remember that she must serve most of the community from her market stall. She's a bit of a celebrity down there with her astonishing mathematical abilities and I guess she knows lots of people that I don't. That must be how she knew he would be able to fix my tablet.

'All's well Mrs. Drachmann. I just need Alexa for a few minutes. I hope you don't mind. We have a few questions for her that relate to her allocation process. It's all quite routine.'

I listen carefully to these words. If he were standing here because I had done something really wrong, then he would have said so. Rule breaking is a matter for public exposure in our world, not quiet reprimanding.

'I'll have her back shortly, I promise you,' he says to my mother. 'Come on now Alexa. Follow me.'

'Don't worry mum,' I say, pulling my robe over my head.

'Of course not.'

'I'll see you in a few minutes.'

I step outside, reluctantly following the black robed figure now retreating down the pathway.

'Absolutely,' she says.

But when I am almost at the gate, she suddenly runs forward and envelopes me in her arms. Even though this means she must break her cardinal rule of never leaving the house without her robe.

'I'm fine mum,' I say, shrugging her off me. 'Go in or you'll get in trouble.'

Over her shoulder I have seen the curtains twitch in the house next to ours and I know that this visit will be a hot piece of gossip later. But looking at the camera perched high up on the lamppost, I see a red light on its side. Officially, it seems to be still a local matter - the Enforcers do not appear to be watching back at the station or it would be green.

'Where are we going Brother Benedict?' I ask as my front door closes solidly behind me.

'We just need to give you some information Alexa. Nothing to worry about.'

At the end of the path, we unexpectedly turn left. I hesitate.

'Aren't we going to the Sacellum?'

'Not this time, no.'

'Shouldn't I have a chaperone then?'

'Oh I don't think you'll need one. There are several people who are waiting to meet you: both men and

25

women. You won't be alone.'

He strides on, giving me no choice but to follow. As we walk away from the safety of home, I can feel the tension inside me steadily winding up as if I was a clockwork toy. When a sudden swirl of dizziness threatens to overwhelm me, I breathe deeply and stare at the back of the black cloak.

But we only walk past a few houses before he stops again. At this point, Brother Benedict turns to face me.

'Welcome,' he says. 'To my home... and our headquarters.'

'Pardon?' I say. Under my robe, my whole body is quivering now from head to foot. 'I don't understand Brother?'

'Please don't call me that,' he says, smiling, and he opens his front door. 'I'm just Ben.'

Nervously I step over the threshold.

Once inside, Ben removes his official's sash and cloak and hangs them up. I notice three other robes, also black, on the back of the door already. With his shapeless shroud removed, he only looks about five years older than I am. He is wearing a pair of jeans and a T-shirt and he has a shaggy mop of dark brown hair that falls down in a floppy fringe when it isn't being held in place by the skull-hugging hood of the cloak. Most disconcertingly, he bears a striking resemblance to one of the guitar players in Xentricity. I feel quite thrown.

'Why are we here?' I eventually manage to ask.

'Well, you wouldn't take any notice of our messages, so I decided that I'd better come and get you instead.'

'That was you?'

'Sure... well, me and my friends... I set up the communication channel when I fixed your tablet.'

Ben smiles again and directs me towards an internal doorway with open arms.

'What do you want with me?' I ask, not moving from the front door.

'Come inside and we'll tell you,' Ben replies, making further encouraging gestures with his hands.

Slowly, I follow him into his front room. It is an exact replica of ours, but has even less furniture in it and no carpets on the floor. In the middle of the room is a round dining table with three people sitting at it; they turn to stare at me as we walk in. The table looks old and scratched, like something you could find down at one of the community furniture centres. But by the look of the piles of paper scattered on the top, I would say that it is rarely used for serving or consuming food.

'Everyone - this is Alexa,' Ben says.

I hear various hellos, I mutter something similar in reply and two of the three continue to look at me.

'I'm sorry if I frightened you,' says Ben. 'I find I get things done more simply if I use my Sacellum position to assist me. This does unfortunately also bring about a certain level of trepidation. But now that you're here, please relax - this is not Sacellum business.'

'What do you want from me then?' I ask, starting to feel less nervous but more suspicious. 'Why did you send those messages?'

'I guess you could say that we wanted to talk to you about the Flow,' he replies.

'The Flow?'

'Yes... who wants to explain?' Ben asks the others.

'I'll do it,' replies a short girl with bright pink spiky hair, dressed entirely in black clothing that is full of holes.

'OK,' says Ben. 'Alexa, please meet Carrie.'

'Hi,' I reply.

'Hi,' she says. 'Right, well I'm sure to you, the Flow is just perfect isn't it?'

'Uhm... well... I guess that it does everything that I want it to do,' I reply carefully.

Carrie gives a little snort of laughter that makes me feel a bit self-conscious.

'But does it though?' she continues. 'Do everything you want it to?'

I just shrug.

'Have you ever really thought about it? What it does do for you? What is actually given to you on the system?'

I shrug again.

'Well, we have, Josh and I.'

She proceeds to point to a tall blond man who inclines his head towards me.

'He's my twin. And for as long as I can remember, we've been playing around with information from the Flow. Trying to understand it better.'

The blond man nods again.

'And that's when we began to notice that the information on it isn't always the same,' Carrie continues.

'If you do a search one day, and then repeat it a year later, the output is sometimes different,' her twin adds.

'Yes - the facts basically change,' Carrie continues.

I stare at her, wondering if what she is saying can be true.

'It happens quite slowly so I don't think people really notice,' says Josh.

'But what we started to do… ' Carrie adds. '… was to keep records.'

'And there was no doubt about it,' says Josh. 'The information on the Flow varies.'

I look at Carrie's twin more closely now. He is as blond as Ben is dark and has a tanned handsome face. Covered by his robe he would appear to be completely unblemished but here in Ben's front room, I see that most of his body is covered in greenish blue tattoos. Uncloaked, the twins make a striking pair.

'As time went on, I guess you could say that we realised that facts shouldn't really be doing that on a regular basis,' says Carrie. 'And it's started to bug us more and more.'

'So last year, we decided to try to find out what was going on,' says Josh. 'While we were at a Sacellum summer camp at Optimas Party Headquarters.'

'Which is where I met them,' adds Ben. 'It didn't take me long to realise that they were up to something. Constantly disappearing when they should be in seminars, that kind of thing.'

'We were doing some investigating,' says Carrie. 'And…'

'The staff were pretty stupid,' interrupts Josh. 'We signed in at the morning roll call and they just assumed we'd go to all our timetabled sessions after that.'

'But we wanted to see if we could use the opportunity to hack into an official Flow terminal and check the algorithms,' continues Carrie with a glare at her twin. 'To understand a bit more about this universal information that the Party says it provides for us.'

'I followed them one day and asked them what they were up to,' says Ben. 'And the three of us realised that we were having the same kind of thoughts about the Flow. I had started to notice an increase in apparently unrelated flashing images appearing in my searches. I was beginning to wonder about the information that we're being given by the Party and I was really interested in what Carrie and Josh were trying to do.'

'But the trouble was we couldn't find anything,' says Josh. 'It was beyond our basic hacking skills.'

'And that was where Krish came in,' says Carrie, pointing across the table at the fourth member of the group.

The tall thin Asian boy at the farthest end of the table briefly gives me a shy look before looking back down and continuing to examine the top page of a pile of papers.

'Yeah, we watched everyone for a while. We were sure there must be a Flow geek amongst the group who could help. And then we spotted Krish,' says Carrie. 'At first we thought he was just unbelievable at programming and we would have to work out some spurious reason for asking him to help us.'

'But as we got to know him,' says Josh. 'We discovered that he might actually be interested in joining us on account of his, how shall we call it...

disillusionment with the system.'

'His sister,' says Ben quietly in my left ear. 'She was allocated last year and he hasn't seen her since.'

I look at Krish and see that his jaw is clenching as he makes notes on a pad to one side of his tablet. Without looking up he speaks for the first time. His words are soft but his tone is laden with emotion.

'They knew he was a monster and my mother tried to stop them but they allocated her to him anyway. They said that it was a good match.'

In the silence that follows, I think of the Sacellum service last night and Tish's allocation to Lukas. It could have been so much worse.

'Krish became a Sacellum worker so that he would never have to go through the same process,' explains Ben.

'And so that I could try to find her,' adds Krish emphatically.

'But we persuaded him that we could do more than that if he was to come and help us. Do something to get back at the system,' says Josh, patting the boy next to him gently on the arm.

'And then Krish found a second layer of information,' says Ben.

'What do you mean?' I ask, turning to Krish. He doesn't hold my gaze, he just blinks rapidly, his eyes searching out Carrie, then Josh, then Ben. He seems to be imploring them to continue for him. But they all decline by looking at the floor.

'Go on Krish,' says Ben eventually. 'It's your breakthrough...'

Slowly, Krish begins to speak. He stares at his hands, wringing them as if he is washing in some invisible mid-air stream of running water.

'I... I... I found a layer of information behind the one that we see.'

He pauses and seems to be gathering his strength in order to continue.

'Well, I didn't find the information, but I found traces of it still being there. It's possible it can still be found somewhere.'

'We think that it could be the interference information that is sometimes visible on the Flow,' Josh continues and Krish looks intensely relieved to have passed back the baton of explanation. 'Pictures of things that don't seem to fit with searches. That type of thing.'

I find myself thinking of yesterday's tablet crash and the photograph of the old man that I could see before my search results appeared.

'So anyway,' says Carrie. 'That's us. We're just a group of people who want to understand the Flow a bit better and in particular, work out why the facts on it keep changing.'

'And who are increasingly suspicious of the Party and the Sacellum that are supplying this information and who are supposed to be taking care of us,' says Ben.

Now that they've finished, I look at them one by one. They are a strange looking crowd and I'm not sure what to make of what they've just told me. They don't appear to be the kind of extremist radicals that the Sacellum says are a danger to our society, but I'm still pretty sure that the Pastor wouldn't approve of what they are doing.

'But what has this all got to do with me?' I say eventually. 'I mean, it's weird and everything, but why are you telling me?'

'Well, we would very much like you to join us,' says Ben.

Alarm bells are ringing in my head now.

'Me? Why?'

'Because you may have some skills that we'll need.'

'What on earth can I do to help you? I don't understand the Flow. I can't programme a tablet.'

'No, but you're your mother's daughter.'

I stare at Ben, bewildered.

'And so we think you may have the analytical abilities that we will need to work out what is going on.'

'What's my mother got to do with this? She's just a market trader.'

'Perhaps,' says Ben but as he says it, I catch a quick glance between Carrie and her twin. 'Although, your mother has phenomenal skills. You have to admit that she is renowned for them.'

'She just likes to work out puzzles, that's all.'

'Maybe, but she's razor sharp Alexa - and you have clearly inherited her clarity of mind.'

'I don't know about that.'

'As a privilege of my position in the Sacellum, I've seen your school reports Alexa. I know that you always come top in Morals and Philosophy. If I remember rightly, your teacher said you have *exemplary skills in logical deduction*,' says Ben.

'That's just school stuff.'

'Mmm,' says Ben. 'But there's also the fact that you've recently acquired a deep suspicion of the system.'

I look at Ben.

'I have?' I ask cautiously, wondering if this is where I find out that I am in trouble after all.

'I've watched you in the Sacellum. Your face is a picture of disdain most of the time nowadays... when you're not ignoring the Pastor altogether to chat with your friends.'

I'm about to deny this but somehow the words get stuck in my throat. It occurs to me, with a jolt, that Ben is right; I have become very cynical when I listen to the Pastor in the Sacellum. I was always a conscientious member of the congregation until recently. But since I was given my white robe and told that I was to be put under evaluation, I've found it hard to accept most of what I've seen and heard there.

'But what exactly are you asking me to do?'

'For now, we'd just like you to help us collect information. We're not sure, but we think that all the material that we're not able to see is linked together,' says Ben. 'We're keeping a record of the searches that we do on the Flow that generate some kind of interference. We hope that we'll be able to find a pattern in it that will enable us to understand why certain facts appear to change over time. We're asking you to help us to do that. And then, when we have enough, we'd like you to help us work out what it all means and what exactly the Party and the Sacellum are keeping from us. And why they are doing it.'

Chapter Five

THE PUNISHMENT

The room falls silent and they all look at me, waiting for my response. I turn from Ben to Carrie to Josh and then finally to Krish. And then a terrible thought occurs to me.

'This is some kind of trap, isn't it?' I say. 'Who are you all?'

'No!' says Ben hurriedly. 'No... it's not like that at all.'

Carrie and Josh join in.

'No Alexa, we need you.'

'We need you to spot the patterns.'

'Am I about to be taken off for realignment?' I ask, ignoring them.

'No, I promise you,' says Ben. 'Think about it... we've

put ourselves at great risk by telling you all this. If you tell anyone what we've just told you, then we'll be arrested for Subversion before the end of the day.'

'Questioning the Party's information system is about as serious as it gets,' adds Josh.

I pause.

'I suppose so... '

'We're not trying to trick you. I promise,' says Ben. 'We'd just really like your help.'

'I don't know... '

'Well, will you at least think about it? What we've told you,' he asks.

I glance at the piles of paper on the table and run through the outline of their story in my mind. Some hidden material on the Flow? Even if it were true, I'm not sure it has anything to do with me.

'Maybe,' I say. 'I don't know. I want to go now.'

'That's fine... no one is going to stop you,' says Ben.

I make a move towards the door; testing them. No one moves.

'I'm just really not sure I'm the best one to help you,' I say.

They don't reply.

Once I'm in the front hall, I grab my robe, slip it over my head and walk out of the front door. As fast as I can.

A few moments later I'm back in the street, walking home. I keep checking over my shoulder, but no one follows me. Once I'm at our gate, I glance up at the front door. I have my hand on the bolt, ready to shoot it across and return to safety. But then I have second thoughts. I'd rather not talk to my mother yet. I wouldn't know what to tell her. I need to think, so I just keep walking. Past my house, across the Iffley Road and up into the warren of streets that eventually lead to the Cowley Road.

It's starting to get busy now. The first factory shift must be about to start and streams of workers emerge from the rows of identical houses to make their way to the transportation pick up points. They are mostly people in gold robes leaving to earn their livings as state employees in the Party's factories, shops, warehouses and delivery centres. Most of my school friends know they will spend their days living here once they are allocated and trained. Only one or two will end up somewhere else; perhaps given a green cloak and sent to university if they are academically gifted enough. Or choosing to take a black one if they opt to devote themselves to the Sacellum.

But today it's not the future that I'm worried about... more the present. So I just keep my head down and continue on to the park. Headington Park, with its views down over the 'dreaming spires' of the city. It's my favourite place when I want some time on my own. I like to sit on a bench and gaze at the row of big houses whose private gardens back onto the public space on the northern most edge of the park.

Because one of them is where I used to live.

Or at least I think it is.

Years ago I found an envelope addressed to my mother at a house on this road. She gave me some vague excuse when I asked her about it, so I didn't find out any more at the time. But about a year ago, I turned up the letter when I was looking for a copy of my birth certificate. My mother had it stored away in her box of important papers and inside the envelope I found a copy of a 'Certificate of Marriage' for her and my father. Given how evasive she is when I ask her questions, I'm pretty sure that she won't tell me anything more about the house. So I've taken to coming here when I want some solitude and just imagining what it would be like to live in it.

But this time as I sit outside, I barely give the house a second glance. I can only think about what Ben has just told me about the Flow. Can it really be true that information on it changes over time? Or that there is a second layer of information that we can't see anymore? Surely the Party would have no reason to change the facts. Facts must be facts... mustn't they?

Thinking about this, I realise that Ben didn't say what kind of facts were changing or hidden. It seems to me that the changes they've spotted could well have been ancient errors, just being corrected by the Party's technicians. We're always being told that the old Web was full of inaccuracies. That's why the Party had to dismantle it. There would be nothing sinister in it if they were just cleaning it up. And as far as the supposedly 'hidden' material goes, you'd need to be a real Flow geek to help find that. Carrie said herself that they had needed Krish at Party Headquarters.

I stand up and begin to walk back towards home.

No, the more I think about it, the more it seems that I'm not the right one to help Ben... despite what he thinks. I'll tell him he needs to find someone else.

When I get home, my mother is sitting at the kitchen table doing her monthly stock order.

'Lexi! Is everything alright?' she says, jumping up to look at me when I walk into the room.

'Yes, mum,' I say, crossing to open the fridge.

'Are you sure? What did he want?'

'Positive mum. He just wanted to... ask me some questions so that they can make a good allocation.'

I start to pour a glass of orange juice.

'OK, but you would tell me, wouldn't you - if there was something wrong.'

'Yes, mum. Of course I would.'

'And it was just about your allocation?'

'Yes, mum,' I say, getting annoyed.

'OK... well it's nearly time to go to prayers.'

I look at my watch.

'I don't know if I'll go today,' I say. 'I want to see Tish.'

'What?' she says and just as I reach the door, she shuts her order book with a sharp snap. I stop.

'Hold on a minute... what do you mean - not going?'

'It's not compulsory on a Saturday morning,' I say.

'No, but you usually go with me,' she adds.

I study her face. She looks genuinely scared.

'OK, I'll come with you,' I relent. 'I'll go to Tish's from there. Happy now?'

'Please don't use that tone. You have no idea how important it is that we don't antagonise the Pastor.'

'Why don't you tell me then mum?' I blurt out before

I can stop myself. 'Tell me why it is so important that we don't when plenty of other people seem to get away with it on a Saturday. I know Tish and her family won't be there.'

For a moment I really think she is going to tell me something - something that will explain why we have to be so perfect, all the time. But then I see the shutters come down and I hear the usual response.

'It just is. Now have some breakfast. A glass of orange juice isn't enough for anyone.'

An hour later and I am sitting on a bench down the road from the Sacellum with my head in my hands. I tell myself to breathe slowly: in, out, in, out. As the nausea subsides, I stagger to my feet and begin to walk as quickly as my shaking legs will take me. I need to get to Tish's house. I need to be somewhere beautiful and away from the horror that I have just been forced to witness.

It all started when the Pastor stood after our first prayer. His eyes were narrowed as he scanned the congregation and his slack jowls wobbled as he worked his way into a frenzy of indignation: calling us all ignorant sinners and heathen wastrels. He was in one of his most vindictive moods.

Having reminded us of the sacrifice that Nathaniel Jefferies made in bringing the Creator's message to us and of the debt we owed him, he proceeded to detail specific sins that we had committed. I knew he was building up to something big and indeed, his final flourish was to announce that he had been given some information by one of the community about a neighbour... a banned book had been discovered.

The whole congregation had gasped. But then he called out the name of the family in whose house the book had been found; the Mansours who run the pet shop. And I started to breathe more easily. Mr. Mansour is such a kind man and I don't think he's ever done anything wrong in his life. I was sure that it was some kind of mistake; that the judgement would merely be a little routine humiliation. And so I was just embarrassed rather than worried when he and his entire family went to stand on the altar steps to apologise for their blasphemy.

But as the Mansours were about to return to their seats, I happened to be still watching the Pastor. He was revelling in their shame, positively glowing with his own power. And all of a sudden, his expression changed; it hardened to pure aggression. Before they could take more than a step or two back towards the safety of the crowds, he held up his hands.

'STOP!' he yelled. 'That was pathetic. Do you expect the Creator to consider *that* an apology?'

The Mansours froze, staring at him from the centre aisle of the Sacellum.

'I can see that what is required here is a proper punishment,' he told them, before turning to face us. 'Something that will serve as a warning to you all.'

My heart started to pound then in anticipation of his next words.

'Do you not value the sacrifices that have been made in your name? Do you dare to treat this Sacellum as if it were nothing? We rescued you! When you were at the mercy of thieves and in thrall to alchemists and their false hope. When you had forgotten who made you and who could save you. We came here and we reminded you. Showed you how to live according to the Creator's wishes. You all need to remember that.'

And before we knew what was going on, the Pastor sentenced each of the Mansours to a dozen lashes, right there and then in the Sacellum.

It was bad enough when Mr. Mansour and his wife were tied up but I couldn't watch when their little boy was dragged up to the frame. He must only be about ten and he cried out for his mother as they strapped his arms to the wood. And because the Pastor ordered them left tied up for us to stare at on our way out, his mother couldn't even comfort him afterwards. She couldn't reach his hand or stroke his head or anything. I thought I was going to be sick.

'I just wanted to help my brother,' Mr. Mansour had pleaded when he was given the sentence. 'His little girl is so ill and I found the book on a junk stall. It had some suggestions for how to bring down a fever.'

'Silence,' roared the Pastor. 'Prayer would be enough to drive out the demons that are making her ill. You should have come to me.'

'But we have been praying for days and she is getting worse,' said Mrs. Mansour, trembling as she spoke up bravely in support of her husband. 'We only wanted to see if there were some herbs we could use.'

'Piety is the only way to rid the girl's body of the sickness in her soul. The Creator is the only one who can make her better. It's about time you learned that the hard way.'

After the beatings, the Pastor set fire to the book. Once it had turned to ash on the Altar steps, we were allowed to leave. There was silence from the congregation as we filed out, accompanied only by the sound of the boy's sobs echoing around the emptying Sacellum.

And now I'm trying to stop myself feeling ill so that I can get to Tish's house and forget this misery.

Tish lives in one of the oldest buildings in Oxford: the Warden's residence at Dartford College. Her father was given it as his home when he was made the local Optimas Party leader and I always love spending time there, because it's so different from our little terraced house. There are beautiful gardens and courtyards and the rooms of the Lodge are ornately furnished and exquisitely decorated with old tapestries and paintings by famous artists.

I get there in record time and knock on the huge wooden door.

'Ah Miss Alexa,' says Peters, the stuffy butler, when he opens the door. 'You may not find anyone up yet I'm afraid. There was much celebration last night on account of the allocation you know.'

'Tish won't mind if I wake her,' I say and push gently past his tactically positioned body to make for the wide, sweeping staircase in the far corner of the hallway.

'I dare say she won't. You can tell her that her husband-to-be has phoned and will be here to have his first appointment with her at eleven o'clock. Perhaps she will come down before then for some breakfast?'

'I'll tell her,' I call and I race up the stairs to the first floor landing.

So this is it then. The way it will be from now on. No more hanging around all day, shopping and gossiping about everyone at school. Now I will get squeezed in between visits from Lukas.

'Tish' I say quietly having first knocked on her door.

'Lexi? Is that you?'

The door is thrown open and Tish hugs me tight to her as she pulls me into her bedroom. She is still dressed in her pyjamas, her normally perfect hair a bird's nest of tangled curls and her gorgeous coffee coloured skin all blotched and red around her eyes.

'Oh you don't know how happy I am to see you. You have no idea.'

'Well the feeling's mutual. How are you feeling today?'

'Numb I think. It still hasn't sunk in properly.'

We walk over to her bed and sit close together, still holding hands.

'I know. I keep forgetting it and then remembering it and then it's a shock all over again,' I say.

'Exactly. Even last night when mum and dad gave me a dinner in honour of the announcement, I kept forgetting what it was that we were celebrating. Crazy, isn't it?'

'Well, not really. It wasn't your decision was it? So it'll take a long time I reckon, for you to remember that it's been made.'

'I guess that's it.'

'Have you found out anything about him?'

'Not really. My dad just keeps going on about what a good match it is. His family are considered very pure apparently.'

I think about Lukas' visit to my house. Initially, I'm not sure whether to tell Tish about it. But I eventually decide that I should.

'He came to see me last night.'

'Who?'

'Lukas Svoboda.'

'He came to see *you*?'

'Yes... seemed to think I could make you think better of him.'

We laugh and Tish gets up and walks over to her clothes closet.

'And *do* you?' she asks me suddenly, spinning around to face me.

I study her unusually serious face.

'Uhm? I guess he wasn't so bad,' I reply, thinking about the conversation in my sitting room. 'He certainly doesn't seem horrible.'

'Oh great... ' Tish says and I can see her eyes filling with tears. '... not horrible.'

'Sorry Tish, I didn't mean it like that. I was just thinking. He seemed... nervous...? surprised...? but, well it's difficult to say when it's the first time I've ever spoken to him.'

'He's not a Flow geek then?' she asks me.

'No, I don't think so.'

'It's just I've never seen him at a Screening Lexi. And once I realised that last night, it's all I can think about...whether he's some dire Flow geek.'

'No, I really don't think he's a Flow geek Tish.'

'Good because I couldn't stand it. I just couldn't.'

'I know,' I say. 'He seemed quite ordinary really.'

I can see from her face that I am not making things better; ordinary is not something that is usually tolerated in Felix Canter's household. And I wonder again why Tish was allocated to Lukas.

'There was a terrible punishment at the Sacellum this morning,' I say, to change the subject. 'Lashes - it's a good thing you weren't there, it was horrible.'

'Who was it?' Tish says although she has a far away look in her eyes.

'The Mansours.'

'The pet shop guy,' she says vaguely. 'But he's never been in trouble before.'

'I know. Just because the Pastor was in a bad mood I think.'

'I was only at his shop yesterday. He has these amazing parrots. I was walking past and I saw them in the window. I went in and his son showed them to me. They were this gorgeous deep blue colour – like that colour we used in art class.'

'Oh, I know... Majorelle blue. How beautiful... well, apparently Mr. Mansour's niece is ill and they were trying to find some ideas for how to bring down her fever. It seems they used a book of remedies and someone saw them with it.'

'You're kidding. He's such a devout man, I'm surprised they got lashes for that.'

'I know. But the Pastor gave us the lecture on *small actions have bigger consequences'*.'

'I guess that's right', says Tish, reaching for the handle on one of the doors to her enormous walk-in wardrobe.

'Is it Tish?' I reply. 'I don't really see how a small thing like trying to bring down a child's fever could lead to people denying that the Creator exists.'

'Well, that was what happened, wasn't it?' Tish replies as she opens the other side. 'Before the Collapse.'

'I know that's what the Sacellum says happened,' I mutter. 'I'm just saying it doesn't make a whole lot of sense to me.'

Tish has started to choose her clothes for the day now. I watch her. Although she is still talking to me, I can see that she is only half listening. She pulls out a series of skirts and tops and wrinkles her nose at each one. Her mind is clearly elsewhere; I suppose she can't imagine how horrible it was to see the Mansours get punished. And I guess she's going to still be a bit dazed from the allocation yesterday. Whatever the reason, there doesn't seem much point in talking to her about it at the moment.

Finally, she appears to settle on an outfit and has just laid it out on her bed when we hear a quiet knock at her door. Mrs. Canter cranes her head around the frame.

'Laetitia, are... oh, hello Alexa. How are you?'

'Fine thanks Mrs. Canter. How are you?'

'What is it mum?' interrupts Tish and her mother

looks briefly annoyed but quickly wipes this expression away to smile indulgently at her impatient daughter.

'I just thought you should get ready. Lukas will be here in a few minutes.'

'I'll go Tish. Call me later?'

'Definitely,' she says and gives me a huge hug. 'Thanks Lexi.'

'No problem, it'll be better than you thought. I'm sure of it.'

'I hope so.'

Chapter Six

THE REVELATION

I don't feel like going home yet. I think I'll go and do a bit of window-shopping: not the same without Tish, but still better than getting another grilling from my mother about Ben's visit.

Stepping through the small door that is cut into the main gate of Dartford College, I hear a young man in a green cloak shouting.

'Tours of the Colleges Ladies and Gentlemen! Tours of the Colleges! Leaving every hour, on the hour!'

He's handing out leaflets to people as they pass, although most end up tossed into the rubbish bin fifty metres further up the street. It is only visitors from other towns and cities that ever take these tours and there are never many of them around. Occasionally I see someone who looks as if they've come from further away - from one of Nathaniel Jefferies' other communities overseas. But I can't believe the student would make much money giving these tours.

As midday approaches, the city is humming with activity. Cornmarket is covered with cyclists. Single people on rickety old delivery bikes or smarter racing models. Couples on tandems. I even spot an amazing contraption which is transporting a mother and three of her children; two sitting low to the ground in a box attached to the front of the frame and one on an extension out at the back. The sound of bicycle bells accompanies me as I head towards the Covered Market.

There has been a Covered Market in Oxford for centuries and I love spending time here. Probably because I basically grew up in the alleyways between the stalls - running around from my mother's fruit and vegetable stand to visit all the other traders. We're a close-knit group because everyone relies on the money they make here to feed their families. Sometimes street markets spring up out in the city when farmers exceed their quotas at harvest time. They seize the chance to make some quick cash, but this causes nothing but trouble for the regular stallholders like my mother.

'Lexi!'

I turn to my left to see a round, red faced man wearing a stripy red and white apron over his silver cloak. Above his head is a large sign: Sweet Nothings. He offers me a plate and from it I take a soft piece of delicious clotted cream fudge - his speciality.

'Thanks Frank. How are you?' I ask. 'How's business?'

'Could be worse,' comes his standard reply.

As the soft confectionery begins to melt on my tongue, I'm distracted by the sound of shouting, over to one side of the market. The shoppers are staring at a man who is gesticulating and waving what looks like a rolled up sheet of paper. But when he begins to ask them questions, they all look away, put their heads down and take a wide path around him. He is attempting to thrust something into the hands of those who are closest to him but no one takes his offerings. Some poor mad old beggar probably. On the whole, poor people are looked after well at the Sacellum, but there are still some who turn down the Party's offers of help.

Looking the other way myself, I see Mr. Jacobs the fishmonger catching some unsuspecting customer in one of his all-too-successful negotiations. I smile to myself, wave goodbye to Frank and continue walking.

The market is teeming with people. Saturdays are always busy. On both sides of me are stalls, with items stacked on the floors, in baskets, on shelves and sometimes hanging from the rafters. Books, clothes, shoes, fish, meat, cakes. You name it there is a stall that sells it here. It's a riot of colour when the stallholders are ready for the day to begin. But when the shoppers arrive in their robes of every hue I reckon it's the most vibrant place on the planet. In fact, sometimes when I was younger, I would walk around the warren of pathways pretending I was a spice trader in a bazaar in Constantinople or a salt merchant in a souk in Marrakech.

I can smell the sweet aroma of cookies emerging from the ovens at Humble Pie and head towards it, skirting wide around the butcher's shop. That always has a rather less pleasant smell emanating from it, with its braces of dead pheasants hanging down at the front and tubs of chopped offal on the counter at the back.

'Double chocolate chip Lexi?' asks Adam from behind his counter when I finally arrive at the bakery.

'Of course,' I say and smile as I exchange some coins for a bag with a still warm cookie nestling inside.

But even the sight of so many old friends cannot really cheer me up today. And when I reach the exit that leads to the High Street I take it.

As I am leaving, a group of Enforcers in yellow robes sweep in off the street and swipe at a piece of paper stuck up on the wall near the entrance. They leave it in tatters, and I watch as they move further into the market and come to a halt in front of a second one. For some reason I think about the crazy man shouting inside. If by some chance he is responsible for these posters, I hope for his sake that he has moved on already. Someone is bound to tell the Enforcers about him any minute.

'We need to tell the Pastor,' says the tallest man.

'I don't suppose the camera will have caught whoever did it,' says his colleague as he points at the surveillance camera and then rips the piece of paper in two. 'They're far too clever for that.'

But no one will need to read the poster to know what it will say. They are always the same; *'Having doubts?'* or *'Need answers?'* Propaganda notices from Scientia.

It occurs to me that I've never really considered their questions very seriously before. But now that I do, I am struck that they are very similar to those raised by Ben and the others this morning. Could they be part of this group? Of Scientia? When I was with them, I was most concerned that they might be working on behalf of the Sacellum; trying to trick me into revealing I was a doubter. A kind of test before my allocation.

But what if I was right last night when the messages came through, and *they* are the doubters? If that's the case, then deciding whether to help them is a bigger decision than I'd thought. But I can't deny, when I see things like the punishment this morning, I do start to have concerns about some aspects of my life.

I leave the Enforcers to their discussions and walk out of the market towards the main shops on the High Street, unable to shake the events in the Sacellum from my mind.

And then in a moment of clarity, I decide I should go and see the Mansours. Show them I am thinking of them. Of course, I won't be able to say anything negative about the Pastor and his sentence, but I want them to feel some support.

Just as I am about to walk up Turl Street to their pet shop, I feel a tap on my shoulder.

'Hi Lexi,'

'Oh... hi, Lukas.'

'Are you OK? You look worried.'

Lukas is pushing his bicycle and I notice he is very smartly dressed.

'Yes, well no, not worried, more upset. I'm just going to see the Mansours at the shop. Were you in the Sacellum this morning?'

'No... but I heard about it. It seems so unlikely that they would have done anything wrong.'

Over Lukas' shoulder I see that we have drawn the attention of one of the Enforcers who has left the market. He must have seen Lukas touch me. I keep one eye on him as we talk.

'It was terrible,' I say. 'I just thought I would go and pet some of the animals and see if their little boy is OK.'

'Would you mind if I came too?'

'No - I guess not. But aren't you supposed to be at Tish's for your first appointment?'

'Yes, but she called to put it off for half an hour so I've got time.'

I look again at the man in the yellow cape standing off to my right. I see him take out a tablet and am pretty sure he is about to record us. But we're not touching, we're just talking.

'That would be great Lukas. Thank you,' I reply, determined not to be intimidated.

When we get to the pet shop, we find it open as usual and I see the three big blue parrots in a large cage in the window. They are squawking noisily and a crowd of children stare at them through the glass, laughing at the birds pecking at one another, hanging upside down or nodding their heads at their audience. Lukas and I walk in. Mr. Mansour is alone at the counter.

'Mr. Mansour?' I say and leave Lukas watching the

birds.

'Hello miss, what can I do for you today?' he says with a bright smile and a slight bob of his head.

'I just wanted to ask after your son. Is he alright?'

'Thank you, yes miss he is all right. My wife is looking after him.'

The shopkeeper is looking a little nervous now.

'And your niece? How is she?' I ask.

The expression on his face alters completely. I've gone too far; he doesn't know me, so he won't know if his answer might get him into more trouble. And I daren't make it crystal clear that I think he was treated shamefully. So for a few minutes we dance around the subject while beads of perspiration appear on his forehead and his eyes dart towards the door. Realising that I have made a mistake in even trying to speak to him, I make my excuses and go to find Lukas.

'Come on,' I say rather petulantly. 'I've said my bit.'

'I'm sure it helped Lexi. It was kind of you.'

'Oh I don't know. What use are words? None really.'

I'm angry now and when I see the yellow-cloaked figure waiting opposite the shop, I am very close to going over and asking him what it is that I have actually done to warrant his presence.

'I guess I better be heading over to Laetitia's house,' Lukas says, checking his watch.

'Call her Tish Lukas,' I snap. 'She hates her full name. Or at least when you are talking to me about her.'

He smiles and grabs a set of earphones that have been resting around his neck while we were in the shop.

'What are you listening to?' I ask, feeling guilty for

taking out my anger on him.

'Uhm, nothing actually.'

'What?'

'I'm listening to nothing with the help of these earphones.'

'What on earth does that mean?' I say.

'Oh, don't worry about it; I have a problem with my hearing, that's all.'

'What kind of problem?'

'It's nothing,' he says and I almost drop the subject. But he doesn't actually sound as if he really wants me to.

'Go on Lukas. What kind of problem?'

There is a long pause.

'Basically I hear all sorts of noises that other people can't hear; that's it really. My father got me these headphones from his factory... to help. The men on the lathes use them to stop their ears getting damaged by the machine noise. They kind of cancel out the noises for me.'

'What kind of noises?'

'High pitched ones usually.'

'Do you hear them all the time?'

'No, it's only at certain times really... in the Sacellum quite a lot... and if I am listening to concerts on the radio,' he says. 'I wear the ear protectors outside in case I get a sudden burst near a community wifi transmitter.'

'Weird.'

'Yes, but I've got used to it... and these help,' he says and he adjusts the earphones. 'But, it's the reason I don't go to Screenings. I can hear high-pitched squeals over the top of the soundtrack.'

'That must be horrible.'

'It's pretty annoying, yes.'

'Funny... I wondered why I'd never seen you there. And there was me thinking you were at home Flow riding.'

'Hardly. I use the Flow as little as possible,' Lukas says abruptly.

This astonishes me. Carrie had been right earlier; the Flow is my connection to the world. I couldn't imagine being without it: no music, no concerts, no way to keep in touch with my friends.

'Why don't you use it?' I say.

'I just don't... like it. Something about it isn't... right.'

'What do you mean 'not right'?' I ask, immediately thinking of Ben and the others.

He pauses and when he continues, he is choosing his words very carefully.

'Oh, I don't know. Occasionally when I search on it, I only get half the information that I think I should.'

'OK,' I say equally slowly.

'Sometimes it's just a feeling I have. But other times, I absolutely know that there is missing information; things I learned in school when I was much younger which don't seem to come up in the search any more.'

I can't believe this. After everything that Ben and the others said earlier; here is someone else who has noticed problems with the Flow.

'Perhaps you aren't remembering it right?' I suggest.

'No, it can't be that,' Lukas says with conviction. There is an enormous pause and he gazes around us before he speaks. Luckily, the Enforcer has found someone else to hassle.

'I've never really told anyone this before,' he says eventually. 'But I don't think that you'll tell anyone.'

'Tell anyone what?'

'I'm not really sure what to make of it myself actually, but I think other people would definitely feel threatened by it. And it may get me into serious difficulty with the Pastor.'

'What is it? You're intriguing me now Lukas. I promise I won't tell.'

'Well, you see, I have an unusual ability... '

I stare at him, eyes wide and nod my head a couple of times in what I think is an encouraging manner.

'... to do something that other people, like the Pastor for one, may not appreciate.'

'What kind of ability?'

'My memory.'

'What about it?'

'Uhm... I suppose you'd say I have a *photographic* memory. I can remember almost everything I've ever seen.'

I consider this for a minute. It doesn't seem so bad.

But then I remember the Pastor and his insistence that we treat him as the only true messenger: relaying instructions directly from the Creator. The Pastor instructs us how to think about the past, live the present and prepare for the future. No one ever seems to challenge his stories about the past. If someone even hints that they doubt his version of how our society came to nearly destroy itself before the arrival of the Optimas Party and its religion, they are tortured until they recant. I can't imagine him tolerating someone in the community who he knew could not only recall the past but who could do so with total accuracy. What if they remembered something that *didn't* agree with his version of events?

'It used to be a party trick of my parents when I was only about two or three. I could memorise pages of books; encyclopaedias, that kind of thing. And I never forgot details of people and places that we went to. But as I got older, they realised that it would be better to hide such an ability and they told everyone that I had suddenly stopped being able to do it.'

'So you remember things as if you just saw them?'

'Well, I don't know if you would describe it exactly like that but I can remember an awful lot of stuff. I rarely forget anything. And that's why I really notice when stuff goes missing from the Flow.'

I am speechless.

'You think I'm completely crazy, don't you? Are you going to tell Tish that now?' Lukas says with a face like a reprimanded puppy. 'I shouldn't have told you.'

This is, of course, not what I am thinking. I am thinking that this is my moment to confide in Lukas about my meeting with Ben - to tell someone about the invitation to join his group. I couldn't involve my mother because I knew she would worry and I couldn't involve Tish earlier as she had other things on her mind.

But can I involve Lukas Svoboda? A boy that I hadn't even spoken to until twenty-four hours ago. But who has just unwittingly revealed to me that he would be the perfect person to ask.

Chapter Seven

THE OLD MAN WITH THE BEARD

'Lukas!' I call out.

It's late afternoon now and I'm sitting on the wall near our front gate, waiting. I'm not sure he's heard me, but then I see him look backwards to check for cars. When the road is clear, he steers his bike towards me.

'Thanks for coming back.'

'Will you answer me now?' he says, dismounting. 'Do you think I'm crazy? I've been worrying about it since this morning.'

'No, of course I don't. I'm sorry if I didn't say that earlier. I just need you to meet someone.'

'So you won't tell Tish?' he says, looking so relieved it would appear that I have taken the weight of the world off his shoulders.

'I promise I don't think you're crazy Lukas, and I certainly won't tell Tish any of this. But you can't tell her anything that you are about to hear either.'

He looks at me, confused.

'Because of her dad... who he is,' I say.

Lukas hesitates.

'Well, I've never told anyone what I told you this morning, so I'm sure I can keep this a secret,' he says. 'Whatever it is.'

'I hope you still feel that way once you hear the rest of it,' I say and we walk the short distance to Ben's front door together.

'Why are we stopping here?' Lukas asks.

'This is where Ben lives.'

'Ben?'

'He'll explain things better that I can.'

'Lexi... just so that I know. Could this get us in real trouble with the Party or the Sacellum?'

'Pretty much either or both, yes. Do you mind?'

Lukas seems to be contemplating the question, and for a terrible moment I am sure he is going to say 'yes' and report me. But then I see a different look cross his face; like the one he gave me just before he told me about his hearing and his memory, and then I know he is still willing to trust me. I knock at the door.

Ben opens it.

'Alexa! I didn't expect to see you again so soon,' he says and then he looks at Lukas. 'Everything OK here?'

'Yes, don't worry Ben,' I reply. 'It's just that I've

decided I might want to get involved.'

'You might?' Ben says. 'Fantastic! We need you.'

'Well, I don't know about that, but after this morning in the Sacellum, I've decided that I would like to find out a bit more about what it is you're doing. There was no reason to treat Mr. Mansour like that.'

'I heard about it,' says Ben.

'It was completely over the top...' I reply. 'But Ben... if I join you... I need to know.'

'Yes? What?'

'Are you part of Scientia,' I blurt out. 'I just need to understand what I'm getting myself into.'

Ben looks serious.

'I understand. But no, we're not with Scientia.'

I look at him, wondering if I believe him.

'OK,' I say, deciding that for some reason, I do. 'I just needed to know.'

'It's fine. We talked about trying to make contact with them. I won't lie to you. We are, as their posters say, *'Having doubts'*, but they are outcasts and traitors. We are just wanting to understand the Flow a little better. Not overthrow the government!'

I smile, feeling relieved that I am not about to commit myself to some illegal, underground organisation over a few unpleasant events in the Sacellum.

'Thanks Ben.'

Having put my mind at ease, I suddenly become aware that Ben is still staring anxiously at Lukas.

'Oh sorry,' I say. 'Ben, this is Lukas. Lukas – Ben.'

They nod at one another. But as Lukas hangs up his robe, I notice Ben's black one with its white sash draped over it and I remember his comment about the group putting themselves in danger by talking to me. He does have a lot to lose if Lukas or I should choose to report him. I hope I've judged Lukas well.

'Sorry to just spring this on you. But I think you need to hear what Lukas told me earlier,' I say. 'It's not just me who can help you.'

'OK,' Ben says nervously

'Are the others here?' I ask.

'Yes, but we're upstairs now. We thought it safer to move the materials to a place where no one could stumble across them. Even Sacellum workers are not immune from suspicion these days. One worker in Reading was sentenced to death last week when they found some old alchemy manuscripts in his house on a random raid.'

We walk single file through the house, up the two flights of stairs and into Ben's bathroom. Above the bath I see a trap door. Ben points.

'Who's going first?'

'I'll go,' I say in an attempt to encourage Lukas. Having heard my conversation with Ben, he is looking as apprehensive as I felt when Ben and the others explained their theory to me. 'Come on Lukas. You follow me.'

Up in the loft, Josh and Krish are sitting on the floor, surrounded by piles of paper; all moved from the dining room table I assume. Fixed to the roof beams are large sheets of card and Carrie stands alongside one of them with a marker pen in her hand.

'Alexa!' she says with delight, but then she catches sight of Lukas behind me. 'Everything alright?'

'Fine - and please, call me Lexi,' I reply. 'Now everyone, this is Lukas. I'm sorry to just drop round like this, but you need to hear what he told me today. And Lukas, I think you need to meet these people.'

'Alright then,' says Ben. 'Who's going to start?'

I turn to Lukas who is suddenly fascinated by the laces on his trainers.

'Would you Ben?' I say. 'Will you tell Lukas what you told me? I think he will be really interested to hear it.'

'Sure,' says Ben and in the space of five minutes he repeats the story that the four of them told me earlier. I watch Lukas intently throughout and when Ben describes the moment when Krish found the layer of information behind the Flow that we are not able to see any more, I know I have done the right thing in bringing him here.

'I knew it,' he says, when Ben stops. 'I just knew I wasn't wrong. There is so much material that is being removed from the Flow that we used to all know about.'

'Why do you think that?' asks Carrie.

Lukas tells them about his memory and about his remembering information from years earlier that he can no longer find on the Flow. The four of them look as if all their Christmases have come at once. Simultaneously, Ben, Carrie and Josh begin to fire questions at him.

'Is there one particular kind of search that you think is most affected,' says Josh.

'Can you give me any examples of searches that you did which were severely altered from what you remember?' asks Carrie.

'Do the flashing images that sometimes appear actually mean anything to you? Are they related to the searches?' asks Ben.

Lukas laughs awkwardly, seemingly embarrassed by their enthusiasm.

'I'm not sure. I would have to go back and think about examples of when it's happened. I've never thought about it like that before.'

'Can we show you what we've done so far?' says Carrie. 'You could see if any of it rings any bells with you and we can add your information to our sheets.'

'Why not?' Lukas replies.

As he walks over to look at the sheet of paper beside Carrie, Ben comes over to me and slaps me happily on the back. When I see the look of delight on his face, I feel strangely proud to have introduced Lukas to them.

'Brilliant Lexi, brilliant. I knew you wouldn't let us down. I'm so pleased you changed your mind.'

'Well, I hope I can actually do something to help you, but I have to admit I'm curious now. Can I see what you're doing too?

'Of course, of course,' says Ben. 'Add anything to it as well. Have you noticed anything recently that hasn't made sense?'

'I did get a flashing image in a search yesterday.'

'Yes? What of?'

'I was searching a town in Australia, but I got a picture of an old man.'

'Come and write it down over here,' calls Josh. 'We've just started a new list of words which have created interference images.'

He gives me a marker pen and I add my word to his sheet of paper before scanning those above it.

'Immunity?' I read out loud from the list.

'Yes,' explains Josh. 'That was mine.'

'What did you see?'

'It was at work. I'm a lawyer and I'm currently defending a Party worker who was caught altering his daughter's school grades on the system. I was doing a case check to get some precedents for our defence. He claims he has immunity from prosecution because of his position in the Party. And I needed to see if it had been used successfully before.'

'But you didn't get just case information?'

'No, when I entered 'immunity' into the Flow, I had a flashing image of a diagram showing something that it called the immune *system*.'

'How about this one?' I ask. 'Why were you putting 'virus' into the Flow?'

'That one was Ben. He was actually checking out the possible causes of your tablet crash last week. He thought it might be a new tablet virus that some Flow Geek had managed to upload onto it.'

'But when I checked the latest Flow pages on Viruses,' says Ben. 'I had an array of images of these spike covered spherical balls on my screen for a few seconds.'

'Weird,' I say. 'And you have no idea what these mean?'

'No idea. Viruses are just lines of computer code.'

I read the rest of the words on their sheet and none of

it means anything to me at all. Lukas is finished talking to Carrie and they join us by the list.

'These are the words that have caused interference images Lukas,' says Ben. 'Mean anything to you?'

Lukas scans the list quickly and his face appears blank. But then he gets to the bottom and sees my addition.

'Darwin?' he says.

'Yes, I added it just now.'

'The man?'

'No; the city. You know a man called Darwin?'

'I don't know him but he definitely existed.'

Krish has been following proceedings from his position on the floor and now even he joins the rest of us as we stand slack mouthed in front of Lukas.

'Lukas,' says Ben with a nervous tremor in his voice. 'Go on...tell us about this Mr. Darwin.'

Lukas looks at us, and laughs.

'You should see your faces!'

'Just tell us Lukas,' I snap.

'Sorry, well, I can't tell you much, but I definitely remember that there was a man called Darwin. And I think he had something to do with fossils.'

'What, those pieces of stone that the Sacellum say are made in factories in China?' says Carrie.

'Yes, well, no. Because he was alive probably a hundred years ago. Or more even. When there were no factories making stone shapes.'

'So why was Mr. Darwin interested in these fossils?' asks Josh.

'I don't know,' Lukas says. 'This is something I'm

remembering from when I was only about four or five. I went with my mother to a huge building in London. There were enormous skeletons and also some smaller fossils and I just remember hearing her tell me that Darwin had used them in developing his theory.'

'This is excellent Lukas,' says Ben. 'If you remember anything more, will you tell us? Anything at all that you think might be relevant.'

'Sure,' says Lukas. 'I have so many old memories floating around in this brain of mine. It would be quite nice to start making sense of some of the weirder ones.'

I think about this for a moment.

'Why would Lukas think that some of his memories were weird?' I say to the others.

They shrug so I continue to think out loud.

'Presumably because they don't seem to fit with the world that he knows today. Surely these are the ones that we need to concentrate on. To find out which facts are being altered.'

Ben spontaneously hugs me.

'I just knew we were right to ask you to help. This is what we need right now. Logical questions and factual answers,' he says.

'Lukas, are you happy to start telling us what weird things you know?' asks Carrie

As she speaks I am struck by a curious thought.

'I don't know if any of you think this is strange, but have you asked yourself why none of *us* remember this information? We may not have photographic memories, but why can't we at least remember some of these things?'

Chapter Eight

THE SICKNESS

'Alexa?' I hear my mother call as I come in though the front door.

'Yeah, I'm sorry about this morning mum. I couldn't bear to stay anywhere near the Sacellum after what they did. I just wanted to get to Tish's as quickly as I could.'

'I know. It was alright anyway, I don't think anyone saw your reaction.'

I push open the door to the kitchen and just glare at her.

'What?' I say.

'The Pastor,' she says, continuing to peel potatoes at the sink. 'I don't think he or his staff saw you.'

'You really think I care whether they did or not? After

what he did?' I shout.

'Lexi... '

She starts to turn around. I cut her off.

'I'm going up... '

The sound of the Sacellum whistle pierces the air: three times in quick succession.

'The urgent summons,' my mother says and she drops the potato peeler into the sink with a flustered clatter. 'What's happened?'

'How should I know mum?'

'Lexi - don't start,' she warns. 'Come on. Just get your cloak on and let's go.'

Living so close to the Sacellum, we are two of the first worshippers to arrive. But over the next half hour, nearly every single family in our quarter of Oxford sends a representative to hear the Pastor's message. We all wait, shivering in hushed silence in our separate compartments of the cold Sacellum. There is no sign of Tish, although her father makes a dramatic entrance a few minutes after we arrive. I chat with a few of my school friends and we try to guess what's happened. None of us can remember the urgent summons call being issued for years – not since I was in primary school when about twenty-five people charged with witchcraft escaped from detention.

The Pastor sweeps in and strides up to the Altar. The Sacellum staff fuss around at his sides and I prepare myself to hear his latest demands.

'People of Oxford,' he begins, and he raises his arms to the ceiling and closes his eyes. 'The day that was foretold is now upon us.'

I feel a giggle starting in the back of my throat; he looks like an over enthusiastic amateur actor delivering a soliloquy. But as soon as this thought pops into my head, I stop myself. Ben was right – I have to careful.

'The Creator warns us in his guidance to us that if we do not remain vigilant and worshipful at all times, he will return to punish us once again.'

Across the Sacellum, the most religious members of the audience begin to nod in agreement.

'That moment is now, fellow citizens. For we have sinned and he begins his retribution.'

All around me there is confusion now.

'But what have we done?' asks a girl to my right.

'It's not like it was before,' I hear a man in a golden cloak say to his wife.

I don't remember what happened Before, but I can't imagine it was like this. The Pastor's sermons have always told us that normal life wasn't possible at all back then. There were riots and murders and it wasn't safe to leave our houses. Members of the old government had fled they said – taken what remained of the money and left the rest of us to deal with the outcome of their greed. The Prophet says that the Creator punished us because society had collapsed. But it's not like that now. With the help of the Party and the Sacellum, we have rebuilt the country. We have recreated communities and restored the Creator to his rightful place. Why would the Creator be angry now?

'Sickness and plague are upon us... just as it warns in the Book of Legends,' the Pastor yells at us from his pulpit. 'We will fall in the streets and the flames of the Underworld will consume our bodies and our souls if we lapse into our evil ways again.'

We all look at him in stunned silence.

'As those of you who were present this morning will know,' he says loudly and then he drops to a more measured, quieter tone. 'It has now begun.'

I stare at him, confused and then I remember: the Mansours and their punishment.

'Across Oxford, I have seen them,' he bellows. 'People with evil burning in their hearts. The sickness striking people down.'

'What sickness?' asks my neighbour.

I shrug.

'And whilst I have spent the day leading the prayers in the houses of those who suffer, I have now received a sign.'

He pauses. Even the smallest children are quiet as we wait to hear his proclamation.

'A sign that the Creator wishes more of us than this.'

'What?' I hear in whispers all around me.

'Why?' ask a few brave people.

'The whole community will be torn apart by death and destruction if we do not act.'

The Pastor is picking up speed, and volume, again now.

'Act to prove to our glorious Creator that we have *not* fallen into our old ways. We must show him that we *still* walk the path of true devotion to him. Tell him that we have *truly* rejected the evil of the past.'

'We have. We have,' call the faithful.

'I called you all here to inform you that we will now be holding prayers throughout the day and night until the Creator sees fit to forgive us.'

A buzz of discussion begins to spread around the congregation.

'All members of the community are hereby compelled to contribute to this worship on every occasion possible,' adds the Pastor. 'And non attendance will be punished severely.'

'What about school?' a girl in front of me asks her friend.

I think of my mother, having to shut up her market stall; our only source of money.

Scanning the worshippers to study the effect of this decree, my eyes are drawn to Lukas Svoboda in his red robe, surrounded by a sea of boys in white. Unexpectedly, I find that he is also looking at me. I want to acknowledge him, but even a nod or a smile would be considered improper so I merely close my eyes in an exaggerated blink and am reassured when he replies in kind. I am just beginning to ask myself what he must be making of the pronouncement, when I hear a familiar voice ring out from behind me. And in an instant, all other thoughts vanish from my mind.

'Excuse me Pastor,' the voice says again. 'May I please ask you to consider whether our prayers may be better held in private?'

I turn and stare at the mass of people in purple and see them part to allow someone to step to the edge of their group. It is my mother.

My mother has just spoken in the Sacellum. No one speaks in the Sacellum. And not only has she spoken, she has questioned the Pastor's orders. I feel the blood pulsing in my eardrums as I wait for the full wrath of the egotistical maniac at the Altar to descend on her. I struggle to breathe; the realisation that this will be the last time I'll ever see my mother hits me like a freight train.

And then, unbelievably, I hear her continue.

'I do not wish to contradict you but is there not a chance that the sickness will spread further if we are regularly meeting one another?'

'Could that happen?' I hear someone ask.

'If everyone passes it to just two people, then we would get an exponential growth rate, and the community would be decimated within a few weeks,' she continues.

'Silence!' the Pastor roars when some of the audience begin to mutter more loudly. They all know my mother. Although they don't really understand what she has just said, her mathematical abilities are mythical and I guess people will be willing to believe that she is telling the truth. And what's more, she never speaks like this.

I know the Pastor cannot allow her to carry on. And he doesn't.

'The sickness is brought upon us by the Creator,' he replies with an unmistakable menace in his voice. 'And in order for him to know that we are repentant, he *must* feel the power of our prayer from this Sacellum. There will be no more questions. Let us pray.'

I watch my mother carefully. She holds his gaze but

she stops speaking.

Through the rest of the service, I barely hear a word that we are instructed to say. I know the standard prayers so well anyway. Instead, I think about what will happen after the service. My mother has almost certainly already disappeared while I have been kneeling here.

After the prayers are complete, I leave quickly. She isn't under the yew tree at the gate. She isn't by the wall to the graveyard. I can't see her anywhere.

I think about what she said. I've never heard my mother so much as raise a hint of a doubt about the Pastor and his instructions at home. And now she has questioned his orders directly... in front of the whole community... in the Sacellum.

The crowds clear quickly; everyone scurrying home to relay the latest news to their waiting families. Still I see no sign of her. I am about to give up, go home and wait for the inevitable visit from the Pastor to tell me that she has agreed to some realignment therapy when I see Ben approaching me.

'Inside,' he whispers as he passes me. 'He still has her inside.'

Carefully, I creep back inside. I can hear voices from behind the Altar so I crouch down behind one of the loudspeakers near the back.

'How dare you challenge me?' says the Pastor angrily.

'You're making a huge mistake. I can't sit by and let you do this,' replies my mother firmly.

'We must pray for the souls of the stricken. All

together. Here in the Sacellum. That is what the Creator wishes us to do.'

'But we must keep healthy people away from those who could be ill. Until they recover from the virus or whatever is making them sick.'

I have never heard my mother speak like this. With such determination and force.

'You need to be very careful what you say to me Mrs Drachmann. I hope that you are not suggesting that this sickness is anything other than a punishment from the Creator.'

'I am not suggesting anything about the source of the illness. Just how we deal with it.'

'Good, because you know the trouble it caused for your husband when he thought he could intervene in the workings of the Creator. I would hate for your lovely daughter to lose her mother as well.'

There is small pause.

'We can still pray for forgiveness, but just not togeth...' my mother says.

'No! Stop! I will not listen to any more of this,' the Pastor shouts. 'You will remember the promise that you made, or our deal will be null and void and you can be sure that your daughter will truly suffer.'

It is suddenly quiet. I crane my neck to see if he is hurting her in some way, but I can't see anything.

In the deafening silence, the Pastor's words ring in my ears; my father, a deal.

As I replay the phrases, my mother storms past me. The Pastor doesn't attempt to stop her, so I presume that she isn't going to be taken away. Funnily enough, she hadn't sounded scared, so she must have known all along that she wasn't in danger. In fact, now that I can see her, it is clear that she just feels frustrated not to have won her argument. And by the intensity of her scowl, it seems that matters to her very much indeed.

Chapter Nine

THE RETRIBUTION

For nearly a week now we have prayed and prayed. The Pastor has decreed that at all times there must be at least five hundred people in the Sacellum. The curfew has been adapted to allow us to get there, we have been organised into different factions and there is a rota for our worship. My mother and I have been separated like most families, so when I am not praying, sleeping or at school, I rarely see her.

I tried to talk to her after her outburst.

'What were you thinking?' I yelled. 'You might have been taken away.'

'Hmm I suppose so, but I decided it was unlikely,' she had said.

'But why would you say anything at all?' I asked.

'I just felt I had to Lexi. What he is doing is wrong.'

'You're telling me that you don't agree with something that the Sacellum has decreed?' I asked in bewilderment. 'You never disagree with them.'

'No, but... ' she said, '...look I don't need to explain myself to you Lexi.'

'I heard you,' I said. 'With the Pastor.'

'What do you mean?' she said and I know I saw a flash of annoyance momentarily clouding her eyes.

'I heard you talking to him,' I repeated.

She paused and then just said quietly, 'Well I wish you hadn't.'

And that was it. No explanation for what had been discussed. No attempt to explain her out-of-character behaviour at all. I had gone to my room furious and played my music very loudly for hours.

Since then, we have barely spoken; I have concentrated on praying with my faction. I don't know many of them, although Ben is sometimes there. But we have dutifully attended the Sacellum day after day to ask the Creator to release us from his punishment. And yet, over three hundred people are now sick.

I think at first many people hid at home when they became ill. I heard of some that sent family members to their prayer sessions to cover for their absences. But after a few days, the Sacellum staff seemed to work this out. Every day now, the Pastor compiles a list of those who are ill, proclaims them as sinners and posts it outside the Sacellum. To prevent this humiliation, some people are staggering to services to try to carry on as normal.

I don't know how long this can go on for. Last night an old man from Iffley, Mr. Braithwaite, died in his seat as he prayed. I saw him with his wife as they arrived. He looked terrible and the two of them had tried to pretend that he was just a bit tired; but you could see that he was struggling for every breath. As we were nearing the end of the prayer session, I suddenly heard the most terrible moan and he slumped forward. His wife was shaking him and calling his name. She became more and more upset when he didn't respond. After five minutes of wailing and crying, with everyone just staring at them, Ben made his way from the back of the Sacellum to her side.

Gently he put one arm around her and carefully unfolded her fingers from her husband's coat. He spoke quietly and gradually she calmed down. As Ben held her she was wracked with silent heaving sobs, but I heard her tell him that Mr. Braithwaite had been fighting the fever for days. She hadn't known what to do and he wouldn't stay at home in case she was punished.

Luckily Mr. White, the undertaker, is in my faction and he eventually came forward and asked if he could help. He made a few calls and as we were leaving the service, I saw his long black van arrive to take away the body.

Mr. Braithwaite is the only dead person I have seen, but I overheard one of the Sacellum workers asking the Pastor if he had thought about how we would bury so many bodies. People say it is mostly the old and the very young that are dying. But I can't see why the Creator would want the very young to die. I don't understand it at all. The Pastor says it is to punish the families for their sins.

As well as killing people, the sickness has also changed the way our whole community is behaving. Most people have shut themselves up in their homes and are shunning interaction with anyone that they think might be a sinner. People who have been in trouble with the magistrates in the past, families who are suspected of stealing to feed their families... they are treated as pariahs by those who consider themselves morally upstanding.

It didn't take long for the old prejudices to reappear either. The father of one of my friends from school is a money manager for the Party. Up until last week, this was considered such an important and reputable job. These were the people who saved us, who took control of the monetary system and used the new financial tools to gradually restore some of the wealth to the country when the rogue financiers had done their worst. But now, any association with money is a source of concern again. Suspicions that these people have once again started to deceive the public, and are the source of the Creator's anger, have risen to the surface. Now Lottie's family cannot buy food in half the shops in town, they are forced to sit with those in purple at the back of the Sacellum during their prayer sessions and no-one talks to her at school.

The Pastor has been conspicuous by his absence – claiming that he has been representing us at Party

Headquarters and reassuring the Sacellum authorities that he is in control. I haven't heard anyone directly criticise him yet, but I have heard a few rumblings. I think it's terrible that he isn't around more. People really need his guidance.

Hearing about families losing fathers or mothers has started to scare me so I've decided that I need to make peace with my mother. We only have each other, so I don't want to waste any more time arguing with her. I am going to talk to her when she gets home.

'Mum?' I call when I hear the door.

'Hi Lexi. Not in bed?' she asks as she comes into the sitting room.

'I'm fed up of trying to sleep in the daylight. And I wanted to see you.'

She doesn't speak, she just walks over to the sofa where I am sitting and puts her arms around me. And for the first time in years, I let her. We stay this way for a few minutes and then she kisses the top of my head and pulls away. I see tears welling up in her eyes when she sits down beside me.

'Are you OK sweetheart?'

'Fine mum.'

'Not feeling hot or anything?'

'No – you?'

'No, just fine.'

'Sorry mum.'

'You don't need to be. It doesn't matter. Let's just get through this.'

'How long do you think it will last?'

'I don't know. I wish I could say. It's the question everyone keeps asking me. As if being good at maths would mean I could answer that!'

'What've you been doing... when you've not been praying or sleeping?'

'A few of us have been talking to the Pastor about setting up places to put all the sick people.'

'What do you mean?'

'Everyone is exhausted. They pray for hours and then have to return home to nurse their relatives who are ill. If we could put all the sick in one place, then volunteers could go to look after all of them together and their relatives could rest.'

'But isn't that what they used to do in hospitals?' I ask. 'I thought the Party closed them all down when they came to power.'

'They did; when they arrested the alchemists who worked in them. But, we're not trying to set up somewhere to cure people. We're just offering a place to put people so that their relatives can attend Sacellum sessions.'

My mother starts to walk out towards the kitchen and I follow her. For a minute I just watch her, trying to decide how to begin.

'Mum,' I ask cautiously. 'I was wondering. Why did they do that? What did they used to do in hospitals that was so bad?'

She turns and looks at me and I can see her weighing up what to say.

'Well... of course they treated broken bones and little things like the nurses do in surgeries now,' she says and turns to fill the kettle with water at the sink. 'But... the Pastor says that the people who worked there... how can I put this...? thought they were more powerful than the Creator I suppose.'

'Why? What did they do? They never say at school when they tell us about it.'

'It wasn't really what they did,' she replies. 'It was more how their promises made people behave.'

'What do you mean?'

'Uhm, I guess you'd say people began to believe everything was in our control.'

'What kind of things?'

'Well, for example, they said they could design you a perfect baby... or stop you dying ... or cure you of illnesses so you didn't need to worry about how you lived your life.'

I open my eyes wide at the thought.

'Their claims made people think that they didn't need to rely on a Creator - whose rules they should live by.'

'And it caused the Collapse?'

'By the time of the Collapse, everyone was obsessed with their own self-interest and lost any sense of being part of a whole. Money had become the focus of worship.'

'And that's why the Creator sent Nathaniel Jefferies?' I say, looking up at our picture of Nathaniel Jefferies that is displayed, as required, on our kitchen wall.

'Nathaniel arrived and showed us a better way of living. Helped us to put the Creator back at the centre of our lives and understand why we were here.'

'And he was the one who said we had to close the

hospitals and had all the people who worked in them arrested?'

'Yes,' she says, and for some reason, I think I detect a touch of sadness in her tone as she speaks. 'He told us that prayer was all that was needed and that people dying was just the Creator's will. He said to remember that when a person died, they were just making the best journey in the world to live on in the Creator's Kingdom.'

'And after the hospitals, the Party shut up all the old churches and mosques as well?'

She nods.

'They said those religions had been weak. They had let the country nearly destroy itself.'

I think about everything she has told me for a few minutes and am silent until she sits down with her cup of tea.

'Do you believe people are getting sick because we are ignoring the Creator again mum?'

'Does it really matter?'

'Sort of,' I say. 'I'm not sure what to think about anything any more.'

My mother looks at me and, as on so many occasions, seems on the verge of telling me something more, but then just pulls back.

'I know. That's why I'm just concentrating on helping the people who are ill.'

She reaches for the sugar bowl in front of her and slowly stirs a spoonful into her tea.

'What is it mum?' I ask.

'What do you mean?'

'The illness. What is it?'

'Uhm... it seems to produce a fever. Most victims have difficulty breathing too. The worst are the very young children. It's terrible because they become delirious, and they get a terrible cough. You can see their little ribs cages shaking as they nearly choke on the liquid that is filling their lungs.'

'That's so horrible,' I say and then I take a deep breath and ask her the question that has been burning on my lips ever since her outburst in the Sacellum. 'Why did you say to the Pastor that it had something to do with a rogue tablet code?'

'A what?'

'A rogue tablet code. You said to him in the Sacellum that it was a virus.'

She pauses.

'I'm sure I didn't say that,' she says.

'You did. When you were shouting at him.'

'Forget it Lexi. Please. You must have misheard; I don't know what causes it. We must just pray. And, until the Creator decides to forgive us, try to nurse the sufferers as best as we can.'

'But mum... '

'I need to get some food Lexi. Go to bed... you need some rest.'

A short while later, I am lying on my bed. My mother has gone out to pray but my brain is too full of crazy thoughts to sleep. In seven short days my world has been thrown into chaos. People are dying and I don't feel as if

I understand why. I have a feeling I don't know the whole story and that brings me round to thinking about Ben and Lukas Svoboda.

In all the upheaval, I haven't given a single thought to the discovery about Darwin that we made nearly a week ago. But since it's the weekend and I've no school, I think I'll go and see if Ben's at home now. He might have discovered something: something to help make sense of the pandemonium all around me.

Just as I am putting on my cloak, I hear a knock at the door. I open it.

'Lukas!'

It's so nice to see a familiar face and all sorts of questions occur to me as we stand looking at one another on my doorstep. I wonder if he knows what this sickness is? Or knows something about this virus that my mother mentioned?

'Hi Lexi. Sorry I haven't been round,' he says. 'When I've not been praying, I've had to help my neighbour; her husband is sick.'

'Don't worry,' I reply. 'I've hardly been here. But I was just going to see if Ben is in. Do you want to come?'

'Sure.'

When we arrive at Ben's he's just returned from a long stint leading the prayers in the Sacellum. We go up to the attic whilst he changes his clothes and I stare at the list of words that have caused interference images on the Flow.

'Someone's added a new word,' I tell Lukas.

'What is it?' he asks, joining me in front of the list.

'Inheritance,' I read.

'That was me,' says Josh and as we hear his voice, we see his blond head poke through the loft hatch, followed by his hands and two cups of coffee. 'Here - take these, will you?'

'Why did you add it?' I ask.

'Work again,' he says. 'I was dealing with a Will. An old lady had died and her sons were fighting about who would get her possessions. There were two different letters, written at different times and I just wanted to check current legal regulations on inheritance.'

'And what did you get on the Flow?'

'Some strange diagrams that looked like family trees. Only instead of names, they had circles and squares at the junctions.'

'Lukas - any weird memories about inheritance?' I ask.

'No sorry. Not this time.'

Drinking our coffee, we wander around the attic, looking at the information on the walls. I return to finish reading the interference list and Ben joins us.

'I just wish I could see some kind of patt ...' I start to say.

'Lexi? What is it?' Ben asks.

'This,' I say, pointing to one particular word.

'Virus?'

'Yes, my mum said it to the Pastor - when she was shouting at him last week. I'd forgotten it was on your list.'

'She talked about a virus?' asks Lukas.

'Yes, she said the virus was making people sick. But

how could computer code make people ill?'

'I've no idea,' says Ben.

'Ben, you've written here that the interference picture showed a ball with spikes on it,' Josh says.

'Yes, that's what it looked like.'

'Was there anything else in the image that you can remember?' I ask.

'No, it's so frustrating. The images are so brief,' says Ben. 'I just wish we had somewhere else to look for information... apart from the Flow.'

'Like a library,' adds Lukas.

'What do you mean?' I ask. 'The libraries are just full of Flow terminals.'

'They are now.'

'And when weren't they?' Josh asks.

'When I was small,' says Lukas. 'My mum used to take me to this building in town where they had loads and loads of books that you could look stuff up in. It was before the Party put everything on the Flow.'

Looking at Lukas, I have a vague recollection of the building that he is talking about. But as I strain to recall more, I am suddenly overwhelmed with weariness. I sink down onto one of Ben's giant beanbags that are dotted around the attic floor.

'This is a nightmare,' I say. 'I feel as if everything we need is so close, but we just can't see it. Perhaps we're just not looking hard enough.'

'We have such limited information,' says Josh. 'It's like trying to find our way through a maze at night with just occasional bursts of moonlight to help us.'

Josh has picked up a wad of papers from one of

Krish's piles. He is flicking through them while Ben and Lukas stare at the interference words.

'What do you think they did with all the books from the libraries?' I ask. 'I've never really thought about it before.'

'Well, they burned a lot because they were blasphemous, didn't they?' says Ben.

'Yes, but the others,' I say.

'There *was* a rumour that they kept one copy of every book ever written,' says Ben.

'Really?' I ask. 'Do you think it's true?'

'I don't know. There was apparently an underground store here in Oxford before the Party came to power. The rumour was that they decided to keep it.'

'Here in Oxford?' I say, astonished. 'Where?'

'Under the university, it was part of the Bodleian library. The story goes that there are kilometres of shelves underground where the books are stored.'

'Do you think they could still be there?' I ask Ben.

'I'm not sure, but if we need to find some books, then perhaps we should go and see,' he replies.

I look at Lukas and he raises his eyebrows and laughs.

'No need to ask what *you've* decided,' he says.

'We might be able to find it though Lukas. Think of that. Then we could see if we can find some of the information that is missing from the Flow.'

'We might be able to find out what this virus is, when it isn't a line of tablet code,' says Ben.

'And then I might know why my mother used the word when she was speaking to the Pastor,' I add. 'Because I didn't mishear her.'

Chapter Ten

THE PARTY LEADER

'Have you ever been to the Bodleian Flow-reading rooms?' I ask Lukas as we walk back towards my house. Ben has decided that he needs to get some sleep. He has been doing double shifts to cover for the Pastor and so we have left him to rest.

'I went once with school a long, long time ago. I remember we were given a guided tour of a very old part of the building.'

'What was it like?'

'Interesting, I guess. There were rows and rows of wooden shelves where the books used to be kept. Every few feet there were big metal rings on them.'

'What for?'

'Apparently all the books used to be on chains and the chains went through the rings so that no one could walk off with the books. When the library was first built, hundreds of years ago, the books in it were often the only copies that existed.'

'Which is ironic because if there are any books in there now they are probably the only copies that exist too; after all the burnings.'

'Don't talk about it Lexi. It was one of the things that's always bothered me about the Party. When they teach us in school about it coming to power, I've never understood why it got rid of all the books.'

'And I feel so stupid for never thinking about it at all. I just thought the Flow was great and easy and never questioned it.'

'Well, don't beat yourself up about it. Look around you. Who misses books? Why do we need more than the Flow for our everyday lives? We don't. It's only me with my ridiculous memory hankering after something I can remember from before.'

'You – and Ben and the others,' I say. 'You all noticed something was wrong and I didn't.'

'Well, we're doing something now aren't we?'

We reach my house and stop. I automatically look up to check the camera. Red. Good.

'Don't worry; they're not watching,' Lukas says. 'I've been checking it as we walked up the road.'

'It's funny; no one's been watching recently,' I tell him. 'I reckon some of the Enforcers are ill.'

'Maybe... Let's just enjoy it.'

I laugh. He's right.

'So, do you have to go now?' Lukas asks me as we stand by my garden gate. 'Is your faction due in the Sacellum soon?'

'No. You?'

He shakes his head. I look at my house and wonder if I should invite him inside.

'Mum's in the Sacellum at the moment,' I say and we stand awkwardly facing one another. Eventually Lukas breaks the silence.

'Do you want to go into town and see if we can work out where the library might have been?'

'What, now?'

He nods. I hesitate and check the camera again.

'OK, let's do it,' I say.

Walking up our road, I suddenly feel self-conscious about being here with Lukas. I step away from him so that we are walking far enough apart and rearrange my robes to make sure that only my face is visible. I have a feeling that we are being watched; despite the red lights on the cameras.

'I suppose the simplest thing would be to find a map,' says Lukas, apparently oblivious to my sudden nervousness.

'There are a few maps on the streets around town,' I suggest.

Lukas nods.

'We could start with one of those... The Bodleian Flow reading rooms will be marked on it and we might be able to guess where the underground system went.'

When we reach the main road, Lukas and I turn left. Lots of the students from the university live around here and on the first corner is a college for female undergraduates. As we approach the building, we see a gaggle of a dozen or so young women just shutting the front door and striding towards a messy rack of bicycles near to the curb. They begin to rifle amongst the apparently random mess of intertwined wheels and saddles to extract their own. And a few minutes later, Lukas and I feel a whoosh of air on our right, as the whole group streams past us in the cycle lane, at full speed, green robes flying. We both flinch as they bear down on an old man up ahead who is wobbling precariously on an ancient looking rusty old heap. But in fact, their peloton sweeps out into the road and calls cheerily to him as they steer around him safely. He continues on his way, barely moving faster on his two wheels than Lukas and I are on foot.

'So,' I ask. 'Have you seen Tish recently?'

'A couple of times. She's fine. We both find it really hard to know what to say, but I'm sure we'll get the hang of it.'

'You will. She is such a great girl. You're lucky.'

'I had to see her father yesterday and that's what he said.'

'You had to meet Felix Canter? What was that like?'

'Pretty scary to be honest. He called me into his study and I had no idea what to expect.'

'You went into his study,' I say. 'Even Tish isn't allowed in there.'

'Really?'

'No. I remember when we were kids. We were making something in her room and we needed some glue. She got it into her head that her dad must have some,' I laugh as I remember the occasion and our naivety. 'We thought he sat in his study like we did all day at school - making things with cardboard and finger paint!'

'And did he have any?'

'We never found out. Tish went in and he wasn't there, so she was rummaging through his desk drawers to look for some. But then he came in... '

'And?'

'And I heard the shouting from upstairs. Luckily so did her mother or I think she would have got a terrible beating.'

'Poor Tish.'

'Yes, as a result of that day, I've never had much doubt that the nasty rumours you hear about Felix Canter are all true. What did he say to you?'

'He just said I needed to know that she was his most treasured possession and that I must take good care of her. That kind of thing.'

'Lukas – whatever you do, don't ever tell Tish he called her a possession. She gets so angry that he treats her mum like that.'

'Oh I won't. Anyway, I'm not sure that he wasn't just trying to turn the conversation around... so that he could talk about some of his other possessions. You know... to show off.'

'Maybe. What kind of things did he show you then?'

'Oh… loads. The study's full of things that he brought with him from the New World.'

'Go on,' I say. 'Like what?'

'He had this copy of the Sacellum Commandments on his desk. It looked just like any other copy to me but he said Nathaniel Jefferies had given it to him so it was special.'

'I didn't known he'd met Nathaniel.'

'Oh yes; he told me that they came from the same state. Mr. Canter was one of the first followers back at the beginning and apparently that was why they sent him to Britain when the Optimas Party came to power.'

'What else did he show you?'

'We spent ages looking at the paintings that are hanging on the walls in there. In fact, that was a bit weird.'

'Why?'

'Well, there are lots of pictures, but two of them are old Renaissance masters... a da Vinci and a Raphael.'

'In his study!'

'Exactly. Not what you'd expect from a devoted Party employee.'

'Did he explain why he had them?'

'Kind of... he said he thought the painters were a little misunderstood.'

I laugh as I reply.

'Misunderstood! I thought people's obsession with personal wealth and power in the Renaissance was where everything started to go wrong for the Christians.'

Lukas nods.

'We were certainly taught that it was when star gazers

started to ask questions about man's place in the world - stopping everyone focusing on serving the Creator,' he says.

'And Felix Canter doesn't share this view?' I ask.

'He just said he thought that they *did* understand about the Creator and his power; and had been misunderstood.'

'And he really has some of their paintings in his study?' I ask.

'Yup.'

'Wow. I wonder if the Party knows?'

'I guess he could claim that they actually belong to the Warden's house rather than him. But he certainly hasn't got rid of them... which you would think he should have done.'

'No kidding.'

Once we are on the High Street, I can see the tall dome of the Radcliffe Camera peeping over the rooftops at the side of us. From the building in front of it, comes the sound of music. I turn and look up at an open window. The building is a college for men and I can just make out a figure in a green robe sitting in the window looking down into the street below. He is smoking, and the hand holding the cigarette trails out of the window, letting the smoke curl in ribbons around the frame and then on up into the sky. The music is sad and melancholic and I briefly wonder about the lonely looking young man. What must it be like to live apart from your family whilst you study the teachings of the Prophet or how to run the government? The students at the university have been selected as future leaders, but I wonder if they enjoy their life of college feasts and opulent surroundings if they didn't choose it themselves.

The sound of a bus horn draws me back to the street. An impatient driver is expressing his annoyance at a group of men in green robes who are standing in the road just beside his stop.

'Look Lukas - a map,' I say, seeing one attached to the bus stop in question.

We walk towards it.

'Hold on Lexi – I've just remembered,' says Lukas, stopping before we reach it.

'What?'

'On the wall...'

'What wall?' I say, looking around me again at the college wall that towers up on my right hand side.

'On the wall next to the Raphael in Felix Canter's office.'

'Yes?'

'There was an old map... of Oxford.'

'Really?'

He nods.

'It might show the book store,' I say.

He nods again.

'But we'd have to get into Felix Canter's study to see if it does.'

Chapter Eleven

THE MAP

We are standing outside Tish's front door, having spent the last ten minutes trying to come up with a good plan for getting into the study. I knock and Peters opens the door as always.

'Ah Miss Alexa,' he says in the suspicious tone that he seems to reserve especially for me. 'Oh, good afternoon Mr. Svoboda. I didn't see you there,' he adds sycophantically as if to ram the point home.

'Hello Peters. Yes, Laetitia seems to be popular this afternoon.'

'Could I just see her for a moment Peters - before Lukas does,' I ask; trying to appear annoyed at the presence of Tish's husband-to-be. 'I didn't know he had an appointment with her.'

'Oh I didn't,' Lukas adds. 'In fact it isn't her I've come to see. I just wanted to ask her father something actually. Is he in?'

'No, sir. He is at this moment in time at the Sacellum for a Quorum meeting. You may wait for him. We are expecting him back shortly.'

'That would be fantastic Peters. Thank you so much,' Lukas says and he steps forward.

'Can I go up then?' I ask, and without waiting for an answer, I push past them both and take the stairs two at a time to get to Tish's room.

As I knock, I hear Lukas being shown into the waiting area just outside Felix Canter's office. I close my eyes and under my breath, wish him well.

'Tish?' I call and when I hear her squeal, I go in.

'Lexi!' she shouts and literally throws herself at me. She's always pretty exuberant, but this is over enthusiastic, even for Tish.

'Wow! Are you OK?'

'Yeah Lexi - just so happy to see you. You've no idea. My dad's been keeping me a virtual prisoner for the last week. He's terrified that something will happen to me if I go out.'

'I just thought you must be in a different faction to me in the Sacellum.'

'Oh he won't let me help with the prayers at all. He's somehow had mum and me excluded.'

I shake my head with the unfairness of it. But I have

long ago learned to separate the actions of Felix Canter from the intentions of his daughter.

'I wish he wouldn't do it,' Tish continues. 'It just makes people hate me. Like when we first came here and he tried to get me all that special treatment at school. Remember?'

'How can I forget? We'd never seen anything like it. Chauffeur driven cars, different food at break and lunchtime, no punishment when you didn't do your homework.'

Tish puts her head in her hands as I reel off the list, laughing.

'We hated you!' I continue, smiling. 'Or at least the others did. I always felt quite sorry for you.'

'And I'll never forget it Lexi. I can tell you,' Tish says giving me a hug. 'Anyway, tell me what's going on out there.'

'Oh, hardly anything,' I say, desperately wanting to tell her about Ben and Lukas and everything we've discovered but I can't put her at risk like that. And now that I'm here, I'm not sure it is something she would understand anyway. Serious stuff like that is not what Tish and I talk about. 'Everyone's just praying a lot, going to school and hoping they don't start to feel ill.'

'Are you OK?'

'Fine.'

'And your mum?'

'Fine too, although I do worry because she's been setting up a centre where the sick people can get nursed... '

'Actually Lexi, can we not talk about it,' Tish

interrupts suddenly. She holds up a set of headphones. She shakes them a little, smiles and hops up and down with excitement. 'Guess what?'

'What?'

'I've just got some new tracks. Shall we listen?'

I smile, but as I look at Tish, I suddenly feel really sorry for her. Her father's over protectiveness has just forced her into a little bubble. She has no idea what is going on outside these walls. And then when I think about what is happening, I realise that perhaps that is a good thing. First her allocation and then the sickness: I'm not sure Tish is prepared for that much change in her life.

'Brad sent them over this morning on the Flow,' she continues. 'It's a new band that is really big out there. Perhaps we can pretend everything is like it used to be.'

'Great idea,' I say.

Tish and I have a special routine whenever we listen to the music that her cousin sends her from the New World. We wrap ourselves up in these enormous fluffy bed throws that her mum bought her once, eat snacks and lie out on the two sofas that take up half of her room. She puts the music on really loud and we close the blinds and turn out the lights. Normally this little habit of ours is just good fun, but I see now that it'll also provide me with the perfect excuse to slip downstairs for a moment or two. I'm pretty sure Lukas will be in the study by now.

'Tish,' I say as she is setting up the music player. 'How about I go down and see Mrs. Peters in the kitchen? Shall I see if she's got any of that popcorn that your mum gets shipped over? We can't listen to new music without food!'

'Do you mind Lexi? I can go in a minute if you want to wait. I just need to set this up.'

'No, it's OK. I won't be long. I like Mrs. Peters anyway, so I'll go and say hello. I don't know how she ended up married to that crusty old grump but *she's* always really nice to me.'

I slip out of the room before she can stop me and make my way down the stairs as quietly as I can. As I approach the last flight, down into the main hallway, I peer over the banister. No sign of Peters. There is no carpet on these lower steps so I remove my shoes and creep carefully down and then around the corner and across the living room towards Mr Canter's office. The chair outside is empty. And the door is slightly ajar.

I stand outside and listen: nothing.

'Lukas?' I whisper into the crack of daylight between door and frame. Still nothing.

'Lukas?' I say a little louder and then whip my head around to check that Peters had not heard me come downstairs.

'Lexi?' comes the reply and the door slowly opens a little more. 'Quick - come and look at this.'

I enter Felix Canter's study; my whole body trembling like a leaf in the breeze.

It is unbelievably plush and imposing. For a start, the room is twice the size of my bedroom at home. It is flooded with sunlight from an enormous window opposite the door. Even from the doorway I can see that it looks out over the Warden's garden in the middle of the college with its old stone folly and well-stocked fishpond. As I step across an intricately woven Persian carpet of royal blue and intense orange silk, there is an overpowering smell of furniture polish. All the pieces in the room look as if they were made for a stately home and every inch of the antique wood is gleaming.

There are tall bookcases filled with ornaments on the two side walls, each with an old fashioned ladder that can slide along to give access to the top shelves. And then there is the desk. It fills the middle of the room: bigger than our kitchen table, with intricate inlays on the top and ornate carvings on the drawers that make a pedestal on each side. An ancient globe sits in a spinner to the left of the desk and two tall red leather armchairs sit in the space between it and the window. This is a room designed to impress and intimidate in equal parts.

'Look. These are the paintings I was telling you about,' says Lukas.

He is standing off to my left and I walk to join him.

'This is the Leonardo da Vinci,' he says.

'How do they know? I can't see a signature,' I say, examining it.

'No. Apparently he didn't sign his work. Everything back then was done for Patrons who paid for particular items. On the back is a letter that supposedly authenticates it, but I'm not going to take it off the wall to show you!'

'It's probably alarmed. That's the last thing we need!'

'It's good though isn't it?'

'Beautiful actually.'

'Come on,' says Lukas, setting off towards a group of three pictures hung in a group to one side of the window. 'I had just started looking at the map when you arrived.'

We both stand in front of the old brown parchment that occupies the space between two oil paintings. At the top are the words 'City of Oxford' and then the date, 1912. We trace our fingers across the glass trying to get our bearings.

'Here – this wide one is the High Street,' I say.

'Yes, and then there's Broad Street,' adds Lukas, moving his finger along the road parallel to it.

'But there are several Bodleian libraries here – all on the road between the two. I think the Flow reading rooms are in that building there,' I say, pointing to one of coloured squares on the map.

'But in general they line up in a north-south row. Do you reckon that means the underground store runs in the same way?'

'It's a good thought,' I say and I trace my finger in a line up from the most northerly building. 'I bet it goes this way because that would be out of town and there would be more space.'

'It would go under the grounds of some of the colleges.'

'No, Lukas,' I correct him. 'It would go under the grounds of *this* college! And look!'

'What?'

'There! Next to the square marked *Warden's Lodge*, there is a set of dotted lines. See? Very faint but look, they go south, away from the Lodge.'

'Towards the Bodleian,' finishes Lukas as he tracks the lines backwards away from Dartford College. 'The map is worn out in between but I bet the dotted lines used to go back all the way to the library. They must show the underground store!'

Lukas turns to look at me but before he can speak we hear a sound that sends my pulse pounding.

A door slams and a deep resonating voice echoes up the stairwell.

'Peters – can you come and take these packages,' comes the southern states drawl.

I just stare at Lukas – seeing my own panic reflected in his eyes.

We both scour the room, scrabbling for possibilities.

'Get under the desk,' I hear him tell me and I blindly follow his instructions.

It is cramped under here; Felix Canter seems to use the space as an overflow from his desktop. There are mountainous piles of papers but if I can just clear the ones at the back, there will be enough room to squeeze in against the backboard and perhaps I'll be hidden well enough. I pick up what seems to be a sheaf of memos and stare at them. They all look the same, written on Party headed notepaper, the top one marked 'from the office of the Chief Inquisitor'. I see the list of recipients of the memo, including all the big names in the Optimas Party and the Sacellum, and its title; 'High Frequency Disruption of Neuronal Pathways from the Temporal Neo-cortex.' All meaningless to me and I don't have time to worry about his filing system now. I throw them on the top of the biggest pile and crawl back into the depths of the foot well.

I sit down just in time to see Lukas pulling the door shut behind him. With my back against the side of one pedestal, I draw my legs up to my chest, and brace myself across the full width of the space. Now that I am still, every breath seems to puncture the silence. The only other sound is the clock on the desk above me, ticking out the seconds, resonating the march of time through the leather tabletop. I listen for the explosion as Felix Canter sees Lukas leaving his study. I wait: nothing. Then a voice.

'Lukas?'

I can't tell if he is angry or surprised.

'How can I help you?'

A chair scrapes across the floor as its occupant stands and I sigh with relief – Lukas must have sat down just in time.

'Mr. Svoboda has been waiting to have a word with you sir,' I hear Peters explain.

'Of course. Shall we go in?'

'Oh, thank you but that won't be necessary. It was just a quick question as I was passing.'

'Nonsense son, come on in.'

The door is thrown wide open and I can see a pair of polished leather brogues cross the threshold, followed by some battered old trainers. I shuffle myself back even further into the cavity and attempt to keep control of my trembling hands by stuffing them between my knees.

The feet walk towards me, not rushing but purposeful nevertheless. I close my eyes and wait.

'Mr. Canter,' Lukas says. He is sounding slightly flustered and I can hear his softer footfalls walk along the side of the desk and on towards the window. I open my eyes into tiny slits and peer out. The brogues have stopped a little way in front of the desk.

'Yes... how can I help you?'

No reply. The seconds seem to be hurtling on and still Lukas says nothing.

Come on. Just say something. Anything. As long as it stops Tish's dad from looking down.

'I realised that I hadn't asked you where you wanted Tish and I to live after the ceremony?' I eventually hear Lukas ask.

'Well, here of course,' Felix Canter replies. 'Your parents weren't expecting to have you both with them were they?'

'No – no I don't think so. I just wanted to check with you first.'

'Was that it then?'

'Er... thank you,' replies Lukas. 'Yes sir, sorry, I know you must be very busy.'

Come on Lukas - you'll need to think of something else, I think as the feet begin to move again. If he looks down now, I'm pretty sure he'll see me under here.

'What's that sir?'

'What's what?'

The feet have stopped. And now they turn and although I lose sight of them, I can hear them trace the same path as Lukas'.

'Out there; by the pond.'

'The folly?'

'Is that what it's called?'

'Yes, it was built by one of the previous Wardens.'

'Who is the bust carved on the roof?'

'That... oh, William Gladstone. The prime minister; you know the one from the 1800s.'

I have no idea where Lukas is going with this, but it seems to have distracted Felix Canter. I hear him offer Lukas a seat and he begins to tell him more about the previous occupants of his College post. Lukas was right about him. He really just likes any excuse to show off.

For fifteen minutes, I listen to Felix Canter telling Lukas all about the famous academics who have been Warden and the importance of the role within the university and the wider community. I am starting to get uncomfortable and so, to distract myself, I stare at the pile of papers alongside me and begin to read the one on the top. It is the memo from the Chief Inquisitor. I look again at the list of the recipients and see the names of all the most influential men in the country. It makes me shiver at the realisation that I am currently hiding under the desk of one of them. I am also intrigued to find out what kind of things such powerful people discuss with one another.

I start to read the memo.

And slowly it dawns on me what I have found. And that I really need to show it to Ben and the others.

But then suddenly I hear Tish's voice calling my name. I had forgotten about her waiting for me upstairs.

It goes on and on. Lukas is trying to talk over it, but I

am sure that my disappearance and my hiding place are about to be revealed.

'Excuse me, Lukas,' Felix Canter says after about thirty seconds of listening to his daughter shouting. 'I'll be right back. I don't know where her mother is.'

He rises to leave and Lukas goes with him to the door. I can see the trainer-clad feet stop and wait there and then suddenly Lukas is talking to me.

'Lexi? Quick! Get up and get out of here. He's clear. I'll wait until he gets back and wrap it up as fast as I can.'

'Thanks Lukas.'

'Don't thank me, thank Tish.'

'OK, well good luck.'

'Shall we meet at Ben's tonight and tell them what we've found?'

'Yes. Seven o'clock?'

Clutching the memo in my hand, I reach Lukas in five steps, stretching out my cramped muscles. Then I'm back into the relative safety of the Canters' front room. Now all I have to do is explain my disappearance to Tish.

I sprint towards the front hallway hoping for inspiration and see the downstairs cloakroom in front of me. Without thinking twice, I run in. Once safe inside, I listen to the sounds of the search going on outside. Finally, at the moment when I'm sure that there is someone in the hallway, having folded up the memo and stuffed it in my back pocket, I unlatch the door and stumble out, clutching my stomach.

'Tish... ' I moan helplessly and stagger pathetically towards them.

Peters just stares at me.

'Lexi!' I hear Tish call out from the landing above me. 'Are you OK?'

'I don't think I am Tish. Stay there,' I shout. 'I suddenly came over really strange.'

'I wondered where you'd gone.'

'I was just in there,' I say and vaguely indicate over my shoulder to the bathroom.

'You'd better go home to bed,' says Peters, now looking more alarmed.

In reply I groan and cough dramatically. My timing is perfect; at that moment, Felix Canter appears at the top of the stairs leading down to the staff quarters.

'Alexa?' he queries. 'What is going on? Are you sick?'

'I think I might be,' I reply, exaggerating my breathing to imply some fictitious difficulty.

'I'll get you a taxi,' he replies quickly. 'Come on now. We need to get you outside I'm afraid. Tish – get up stairs NOW!'

'But, dad, I want to wait with Lexi.'

'No – get to your room. We can't take any chances.'

And ten minutes later I am sitting in a taxi on my way home courtesy of Felix Canter. I feel terrible for deceiving Tish but I'm pretty sure she'd understand.

Chapter Twelve

THE MEMORANDUM

I'm slightly late arriving at Ben's and everyone else is already upstairs.

'Come on Lexi,' says Carrie as soon as I am up the steps. 'Lukas is being very mysterious. He won't tell us anything.'

'I told you we went looking for books,' Lukas says to her.

I smile at Lukas, grateful for his patience.

'Actually I'm glad you haven't started because before we tell you what we found, I wanted to show you all this,' I say and I hold out the folded memo.

'What's that?' Lukas asks.

'I found it under Felix Canter's desk,' I reply. 'I have a feeling it might explain something that didn't make sense when we were talking before.'

'What?' Ben asks. 'You mean about the missing information?'

'Kind of,' I reply. 'More about why very few people seem to have noticed that the information is missing in the first place.'

The others look confused so I begin to read from the memo.

'...the work was a continuation of work carried out many years ago on the various types of dementia. Our researchers now tell us that in order to maintain the disruption of electrical transmission from the neurones of the temporal neocortex, the subjects must be exposed to the high frequency waves for at least fifteen minutes every twelve hours. If such a condition is met on a daily basis, then the test subjects have been found to have significant memory impairment. Most importantly, the impairment is restricted to episodic long-term memories and does not appear to affect short-term learning or working memory and thus does not hinder procedural learning. This means that subjects can function normally on a daily basis but cannot retrieve memories from a time before the exposure began.'

I pause and look up at the others.

'What! Have I understood that correctly?' asks Ben. 'Is it saying that exposure to some kind of wave stops you being able to remember things?'

'I think so,' I reply.

We stare at one another.

'And who wrote this memo Lexi?' asks Josh.

'It's from the office of the Chief Inquisitor,' I reply. 'I'm not sure if he wrote it but he's the one telling the others about the research.'

'So do we think that someone is using this... whatever they called it... disruption?' asks Lukas.

'They could be, couldn't they?' I say. 'It might explain why people don't seem to be bothered when the information on the Flow changes.'

'But that's... that's... no!... surely that can't be happening?' says Ben.

We all consider the implications of the idea for a moment or two.

'Hold on,' says Carrie. 'Surely if it was happening, then Josh and I couldn't have noticed the changes in our Flow searches? We would have forgotten like everyone else.'

I pause for a minute but then remember what they told me when I first met them.

'But you knew because you kept the Flow searches didn't you? You kept a paper copy of what you'd found each time.'

The twins nod.

'Well, in a way, they would be a bit like written memories, wouldn't they? Having them could have made you able to see how things changed without actually being able to remember yourselves,' I suggest.

'I guess... ' Carrie says slowly.

'But what about me?' Lukas suddenly asks.

'What do you mean?' Josh says.

'Me,' says Lukas. 'I *can* still remember things. I don't write things down and yet I can still remember them.'

'I know... I have to admit that doesn't make sense,' I say.

But then, out of the blue, from his seat on the floor, Krish speaks. He is very quiet and we all have to take a step closer to hear him properly.

'Did it say High Frequency Waves?' he asks.

I nod.

'Go on Krish... ' urges Ben. 'What about them? Do you know what they are?'

'Well, I was just thinking... that they could be high frequency *sound* waves,' he replies.

'But wouldn't we hear them if they were sound waves?' I ask.

'Not necessarily,' he replies. 'Humans can only hear up to 20,000 Hertz. If they were an even higher frequency than that, then we wouldn't hear them.'

Now, as Krish finishes, Lukas begins to speak and we all turn back to him.

'But I *would* be able to,' he says. 'You wouldn't hear them but I would.'

'You would?' asks Ben.

'Yes, I wear ear defenders and earplugs because I can hear sounds beyond the usual range for humans. And I do...all the time.'

'You do?' asks Josh.

Lukas nods.

'I often hear high-pitched sounds when other people don't seem to. I was telling Krish about it when we first met. He'd noticed my ear plugs.'

'But hold on a minute. It shouldn't matter that you can hear the sounds. They should still affect you,' says Ben. 'How come you can still remember things?'

'Because although he can hear them, he doesn't listen to them,' I say, thinking out loud.

I look at Krish and he nods - way ahead of me already.

'He blocks them out with his ear plugs,' I continue.

'And that means I am not affected by the waves and can still remember things,' continues Lukas. 'It's a bonus that I have a very accurate memory but the real difference is that I can still remember things and other people can't. It must be because I block out the sounds.'

'But you know what this proves?' asks Ben.

'What?' Josh asks.

'That someone is doing it,' says Ben. 'Actually using this technology.'

'To make us forget things we used to know,' adds Carrie.

'But why?' asks Lukas.

'That is the crucial question Lukas,' I say. 'I think we need to find out some more about this missing information and then we might know the answer to that.'

'I agree,' Ben says. 'So come on you two, you can start by telling us whether you've found the books.'

'Well, we found a map that we think shows the location of the old underground book store,' I say.

'But we're no nearer to knowing if there's anything still in it,' warned Lukas.

The two of us explain about the map in Felix Canter's

study and about the underground tunnel that appears to run from the Lodge to the Bodleian.

'But the map was from 1912 so we've no idea if anything is still in there,' says Lukas.

'So the next thing is to go and try and find the entrance, see if we can still get inside and find out,' I say.

'How will you do that though?' Josh asks.

'Lexi - Do you have any idea where a tunnel entrance might be at the Lodge?' asks Ben. 'You've been there the most.'

'I know. I've been trying to work that out ever since Felix Canter put me in a taxi.'

'And you've not remembered anything useful?' asks Carrie.

'No. And over the years, I've pretty much explored the whole of that house with Tish. Felix Canter's study was the only place that I had never been and now that I've seen that, I don't think it could be in there.'

'No secret panels in the wall then?' asks Josh with a laugh.

'No – unfortunately. Or should I say fortunately. I wouldn't want to get stuck in there again.'

'I have an idea,' Lukas says suddenly.

We all look at him expectantly.

'The folly,' he says. 'In the Warden's garden.'

'What about it?' I say.

'What *is* it?' asks Carrie.

'A little stone summerhouse kind of thing, built at the edge of the pond,' says Lukas. 'A place to sit and watch the fish swimming I guess.'

'Why do you think it could be the entrance though?' I ask.

'Well, Tish's dad told me that it was built by one of the previous Wardens as a memorial to Gladstone, the prime minister.'

'Yes, I heard him.'

'So?' says Josh.

'Well, when I went on a tour of the Bodleian Flow reading rooms, they showed us some of the old bookcases that were used in the past, and told us that the design of them had been suggested by Gladstone. He was an Oxford University graduate and had suggested these movable shelves on rollers that hung down from the ceiling.'

'And so you think that they might also have built a memorial to him at the end of the tunnel?' I ask.

'Why not? It's just an idea. He was definitely connected to the library so it's got to be worth a try.'

I look at the others. They don't seem particularly impressed by Lukas' idea but something about it seems to make sense to me.

'Was Gladstone a student at Dartford College?' I ask.

'Krish – check the Flow will you. William Gladstone, Prime Minister,' says Ben.

'Christ Church College 1828-1831,' says Krish as he reads from his tablet.

'So there would be no real reason to put a bust of him on a building at Dartford then,' says Josh. 'Unless it *was* in connection with the library.'

'I think it's worth checking out, Ben,' I say.

'I agree,' he says. 'I can't see we've got anything to

lose. When shall we go?'

'Hold on,' says Lukas. 'Surely we can't all go? How are six of us going to get into the Warden's garden and into the folly without being seen?'

'Lukas and I will go,' I say. 'We're the only ones who would have even half a reason for being there if anyone sees us.'

Lukas nods his willingness and reluctantly the others agree.

'Just promise you'll take care,' says Ben.

'When shall we go?' I ask Lukas as we leave Ben's house. It is getting dark and so it must be about time for the lights to come on and the curfew to begin. 'Tomorrow afternoon?'

'What about tonight?' he suggests.

'Tonight!'

'Well, why not?'

'Uhm... the curfew! It's only relaxed for people going to pray.'

'I'm not forgetting about the curfew, but we're going to have to go in the dark Lexi. There's no way we'll get into that garden in broad daylight.'

'I suppose so - I hadn't thought about that.'

'And now's as good a time as any. Isn't it?'

'I suppose it is.'

Contemplating this degree of rule breaking suddenly makes me very nervous.

'Do you want me to go on my own?' Lukas asks as he sees me looking at my neighbours windows, then at the cameras and finally back to my own house. 'I don't mind.'

'No, definitely not,' I say. 'I got you into all this. Anyway... I want to see if there are any books down there.'

I pause for a moment.

'I've never been out after curfew before though... except to go to the Sacellum. Have you?'

'No, never,' he replies.

'At least I wouldn't have to sneak out under my mother's nose,' I say, thinking out loud. 'She'll be at the Sacellum with her faction this evening.'

'So shall we do it then?'

I look at Lukas. In going out alone after dark with a boy that I barely know, I am disregarding every rule that the Sacellum has ever made for me. Rules they told me were for my own protection... But I am capable of making my own judgements about people... This boy is not about to hurt me.

'Yes, let's do it,' I say. 'My mum goes out about nine. I'll leave after her and could be at Tish's house about nine thirty.'

'Perfect. I'll just tell my parents I'm going to bed and sneak out.'

'Shall we meet by the side door; the one in the wall?'

Lukas nods.

Chapter Thirteen

THE FOLLY

It's cold when I finally leave the house and I'm running a bit late. Before my mother went out, I sat in the kitchen with her and she made me some supper. I looked at her face; previously so rounded and cheerful. Although it's been driving me crazy recently, her relentless devotion to the Sacellum had at least always seemed to make her relax and it gave us a pattern to our days. Now, she is pale and thin and has dark circles under her eyes. I'm not sure how much more of this she can take. I try not to think about that now – as I embark on something that would only give her more to worry about.

I have covered myself with an old black sheet. I think it was once part of a table top magic set that my mother gave me for Christmas. But it was all I could find that would shield my white cloak a little from the glare of the lights. As soon as I am out of the front door, I automatically look up at the camera on the lamp post in the garden to my right.

Damn! Green.

I hang back near our front door and watch it for a while. The cylindrical lens is gliding smoothly from side to side, panning the street. It's not just an automaton then. There really must be someone monitoring us this time. And they will know it is not my time for prayer.

But I can't let Lukas down. I'm going to have to find a way.

My only hope is the shadows - I need to find somewhere dark, where the authorities won't be monitoring movements. And the one place that springs to mind is the towpath. I gaze over to my left; in the general direction of the river. At the height of the rooftops, mist hangs in the air. The searchlights are reflecting back off it and it looks as if the world just stops at the end of my road. I have promised my mother that I will never use that route back from town. She says people get robbed... or worse... down there in the daylight. I can't imagine how bad it might be at night.

I am frozen for a few minutes. It would be better to go another night when the cameras are not on. But on the other hand, if I go we might get some answers tonight that will help us make sense of what is happening to the

Flow. And Lukas will be waiting.

There is no choice really.

The quickest way to the towpath is to use the alley between two sets of terraced houses opposite our home. Fifty metres down that pathway and I will be at the river's edge.

I track the camera as it moves across our driveway and as soon as it is pointing up the road for a few moments, I sprint. Once across the road, I dart into the alleyway. And stop; waiting for my eyes to adjust to the dim light, feeling the hairs on the back of my neck stand up.

As I wait, I find that I have the ears of a bat; picking up the faint sounds of televisions in distant houses, of the river lapping gently against its banks ahead of me and then the myriad of nocturnal animals that are all around me. In front of me is the profile of a skinny cat slinking along the garden wall to the left. But it must jump down onto the path in front of me, because it suddenly disappears into the inky blackness.

Above me the small crescent moon gives a little light. And at least it isn't raining.

I can see a little way in front of me now, so I step forward. After no more than half a dozen steps, I begin to jog and then to run. The narrow confines of the alley are horribly claustrophobic and I can feel a vague sense of panic rising inside me. But I drive myself forward and rush towards a set of twinkling lights that appear reflected on the river ahead.

And then I feel the open space again. I am there.

A gentle breeze blows off the river. Standing at the edge of the water, I check from side to side to see what horrors this place will bring. But it is deserted, peaceful even. I don't know what I expected but I almost laugh with relief.

Setting off along the dried mud that forms the pathway, I'm feeling brave, fearless. The path twists and winds with the river. A noisy bullfrog makes me jump with his sudden exclamation in the reeds, but there are still no people to be seen. Sometimes I hear a rustle in the hedges to my right and I veer a little closer to the river on my left but no danger materialises.

And eventually I reach the centre of town. Here there are more boats moored at the edges of the water. Some of the houseboats have lights on inside and I am careful to slow down and creep past them. But all I hear are merry voices and the clink of cutlery, crockery and glassware as their inhabitants wile away the evening; released from the obligations of the Sacellum and prayer and all other establishment restrictions by choosing to live here on the edges of society, excluded and shunned.

Checking my watch in the moonlight I see that it is almost nine thirty. Just before Folly Bridge, I find the short path leading away from the river and into town. It takes me onto the playing fields of one of the colleges. From here it will just be a short run until I am at the gates of Dartford College.

As I leave the river, I feel an almost overwhelmingly intense thrill that I have survived. Although deep in my brain, a nagging voice suggests that I might not have actually been in any danger at all.

When I arrive, I scan the length of the wall in front of me. Just before I begin to panic that Lukas has been taken by a patrol, he steps from the shadows beside a flowerbed.

'I'm so sorry I'm a bit late,' I say.

'Don't worry. But I've checked the door and it's locked.'

Oh no...'

'I thought it might be though,' he says as he fishes around in his rucksack and after a moment or two, pulls out a length of rope.

'And your plan is... ?' I ask.

'I'll give you a leg up onto that wall. If you can get down on the other side and tie this rope to something, I'll use it to climb up and over.'

It works perfectly, and a few minutes later, we are on the other side of the wall, trying to get our bearings. I know the Dartford College grounds pretty well, although I've never actually been into the Warden's Garden. I set off towards it with Lukas following, coiling up the rope as he walks and then storing it safely away in his bag.

We find the old gate and move to one side a wooden notice telling us that it is 'Private'. I try the handle; it turns. I guess members of the college can usually be relied upon to heed the plea on the plaque.

'Hold on a minute,' Lukas says as I set off through the gate. 'Remember how we saw this garden?'

'From the study.'

'Exactly. What if Felix Canter is sitting in his armchair looking this way? We just need to check before we go running in.'

'Good point.'

Almost on all fours, I push open the gate and creep inside. Once clear of the wall I can see across the pond to the house. Several rooms are illuminated. I mentally walk through the house and rotate the image to work out which windows I am looking at from out here; Tish is awake, Mrs Peters must be still in the kitchen and I think the other upstairs room is Mr. and Mrs. Canter's. No more lights. The study seems unoccupied.

'It's OK,' I say in a loud whisper over my shoulder. 'It's dark over there.'

Lukas and I move carefully across the garden towards the dark outline of the stone edifice in front of us. We are about to walk onto the small area of stone paving that surrounds it, when something suddenly comes flying towards me out of the folly. I feel a warm softness on my face, my hair is pulled and twisted and I feel scratching on my head. Trying not to scream at the top of my lungs, I spin around, waving my arms and snatching at my hair.

Then suddenly I feel strong arms grip my shoulders.

'Lexi! Calm down; it was just some bats.'

I gradually sink to the floor.

'Lukas?'

'Yes, don't worry. One got stuck in your hair but it's gone.'

We sit for a moment with Lukas holding me whilst I try to get my breath back.

'Come on scaredy-cat. We need to find that tunnel.'

'Yes, of course, come on... sorry.'

We walk into the folly in silence. I have never felt so idiotic.

The folly is virtually empty. Lukas and I move to opposite ends of the small building. So embarrassed by my ridiculous reaction to the bats, I throw myself into intently scouring the walls and ground for signs of anything peculiar. The moon gives me just enough light to see the outlines of stone benches built around the sides of the structure. But that is all that I can see.

'Anything?' I ask Lukas.

'No, I don't think so. You?'

'Nothing.'

I sit on one of the benches – what an anticlimax. I see Lukas bend to sit on the bench opposite, and he stares at the ground.

'Luk...'

'Lex...' He says at the same time. 'Sorry, you go first.'

'Oh... I was just going to say that I was sure you were onto something.'

'Thank you but I was obviously wrong. Shall we get out of here?'

'I guess so.'

As I stand up to leave, I can suddenly see more clearly.

'Lexi?'

'Hmm'

'It's got lighter.'

'It's just our eyes adjusting.'

Lukas is standing up too and I see him walk over to the entrance. Then he throws himself back inside the folly and presses himself against the wall.

'No, it's not. Don't move Lexi! Felix Canter is in his study. He's staring out of the window.'

Chapter Fourteen

THE HIDDEN LIBRARY

'Did he see you?' I say quietly.

'I'm not sure; even with the light from the study it's pretty shadowy in here.'

I crouch down and creep across to the open doorway next to Lukas. Felix Canter is silhouetted against the light in his study and he is staring across the pond straight towards us.

'If he'd seen us, he wouldn't still be standing there,' I say.

We watch him for a while. He is talking on the phone and begins to pace up and down in front of the window. Every now and then, he stops and stares out of the window again - directly at the folly.

'We can't stay here all night,' I say eventually.

'No, but what do you suggest?'

'I don't know,' I say, thinking hard. 'How about we try to get out of here next time he turns around?'

'OK, it could work...'

'Let's just see if we can get round to the back of the folly. At least then we'll be hidden from the study and we can plan how to get out of the garden after that.'

'Right. He's walking towards the back wall now. Let's go!'

Together we dash out of the folly and quickly turn to our right to sprint along the side of the stone structure and towards it's back wall. It's a bit further than I expect and I start to panic that Felix Canter has already turned around and is watching us run. But once we are behind the building and I peep around to look back at the Lodge, I see that he has, in fact, climbed up one of the ladders in front of his bookshelves and is reaching for something.

'That took longer than I thought,' says Lukas, breathlessly.

'I know.'

'How do we get back across the garden then?'

But I don't answer. Because I'm thinking about what Lukas has just said.

I look along the back wall and see a wooden door with rusty metal hinges just a few feet to my left.

'Lukas?'

'Yes?'

'This building.'

'Yes?'

'It seems to be bigger on the outside than it is on the inside.'

'What do you mean?'

'Like you said - it took longer to get to the back than we expected. Inside it was quite a narrow space but out here, it's quite wide.'

'And you're thinking... '

'That what appeared to be the back on the inside, wasn't really the back of the folly at all.'

'So you think there could be an entrance to the tunnel in the space between the back of the building and the back of the seating area inside?'

'There could be,' I say. 'And look...'

I point to the wooden door.

'What? It's just the back d... '

'Exactly! There wasn't a back door on the inside.'

'Come on. Help me get it open.'

The moon is now hidden behind a cloud and so the two of us have to feel all over the door with our fingertips to determine how it is secured. We soon locate a bolt at the top and one at the bottom. But there doesn't seem to be any lock that needs a key. The bolts are very rusty but they move a little as we jiggle them up and down.

For the next five minutes, Lukas works on the top one whilst I try to loosen the bottom. As I am beginning to give up, I hear him grunt when his bolt suddenly moves and then I hear a sharp crack as it hits its backstop. We both inhale deeply and freeze for a few seconds.

'I'll just check he didn't hear that,' Lukas says, and he

creeps back to the corner to peer towards the Lodge.

'OK?' I whisper.

'OK.'

The two of us get to work on the other bolt and eventually it too slides free. Carefully we lift the latch and pull.

The wooden door swings open and we peer into the gloom.

Lukas reaches into his backpack and pulls out a torch.

'You really did come better prepared than I did,' I say.

'Shield it a bit with your hand,' he says as he passes me the torch. 'But we'll need it to see what's in here.'

As soon as I turn the beam inwards, it is clear we have found the entrance to the tunnel. There are a few old garden tools propped up against the internal walls, but directly in front of the door, appearing to plunge down beneath the Folly are a set of carved stone steps.

'Brilliant Lexi,' says Lukas.

'Your idea to look in the folly,' I remind him.

'Come on. Shall we go down?'

'Well, I'm not going back now,' I laugh.

As we descend, I can feel the roughly hewn stairway has become slippery underfoot. I briefly point the torch at my shoes and see that there is a steady stream of water trickling down the steps; making a film across their surface and collecting in the many natural crevasses and ridges. It is cold too and when I turn the light back behind me to look at Lukas, I catch the ghostly swirls of his hot condensing breath in the beam.

After no more than twenty steps, we reach the bottom and find ourselves in a wide tunnel that heads off to our left. It's ceiling is high enough for us to stand and the walls look rubbed smooth. There is a framework of wooden supports at regular intervals and the water on the floor is running in a narrow channel carved at the side so that our feet are completely dry.

'It looks well used,' I say.

'Yes, I can just imagine all those old students in their gowns, sweeping along here,' Lukas adds.

'Coming to do their late night essay writing in the Bodleian.'

'By candle light,' add Lukas and he reaches into one of the small alcoves that dot the walls, scrapes his finger on the base of it and lifts it up to show me.

'Wax?' I ask and he nods.

The two of us walk side by side for what must be about a hundred yards. The air around us smells like a wet dog, the walls are damp to the touch and the tunnel seems to stretch indefinitely ahead of us.

'What if this doesn't actually go anywhere Lukas?' I ask eventually.

'What do you mean? It's got to go somewhere.'

'Well, remember the map? It just showed dotted lines. But they faded out and we just assumed the tunnel went to the library. Maybe it doesn't anymore.'

'It'll go there,' he says. 'Where else is it going to go?'

And just as he says it, we turn a bend in the tunnel and in front of us we see a wooden door. It is about four foot wide, six foot tall and has a curved top. It reminds me of the one in the Sacellum. We approach it and, with both hands, Lukas reaches for the heavy circular metal ring that is bolted on as a handle.

'Here goes,' he says, twisting his wrists. A clang echoes along the passageway. 'It's not locked. Help me pull it.'

We both grasp the handle and lean backwards. Slowly the door swings open. Stepping across the threshold, I shine the torch around us in wide sweeping movements.

'Wow!' says Lukas.

'Unbelievable,' I add.

In front of us are row upon row of wooden shelves. We seem to have entered at the side of the underground room and so we are looking at the edges of the shelving units. Some are bunched together and some have corridors between them. On the ceiling I see complex sets of wheels and tracks above the racks.

And the shelves are all packed full of books.

'It's all still here Lukas,' I say with delight.

'Those must be the hanging bookcases that Gladstone suggested,' he replies and steps forward to push the side of one bookcase that has a wide space to its left. It glides smoothly into the void and we are able to walk now along its length and examine some of the materials on the shelves.

'Look at all this,' I say, grabbing randomly at the neatly filed pamphlets, books and magazines lined up in front of me.

For several minutes we peruse the collection, occasionally removing something to examine it more closely. Many of the newer looking books have brightly coloured paper jackets wrapped around them whilst the older ones are bound in heavy leather and have a strange musty smell. It is awe inspiring.

'Imagine collecting all this,' I say to Lukas as I step back to look at a whole shelf.

But he is no longer alongside me.

In the not quite blackness of the room, I can see his outline in the corridor at the edge of the bookcase. I walk to join him, my initial excitement at the sight of this Aladdin's cave being steadily replaced by trepidation.

'I never thought about how much there would be here,' I say. 'One of every book ever written is a lot of books.'

'I was just thinking that.'

'How are we going to find anything specific in here?'

'I don't know. Perhaps we need to work out how it's organised?'

'Yes, that would help.'

'Come on then. Let's keep walking and see what we find.'

We study the shelves for labels and the ends of the bookcases for markings to see if we can work out how things are arranged.

'It isn't chronological,' says Lukas. 'Or at least, not here it isn't.'

'No, I think it's by subject,' I say when the torch lights up a metal plate on a shelf marked *'Chemical*

Engineering.'

We reach the end of the section of bookcases and the space on our left opens out. It is filled with small desks.

'What do you think they are?' I ask, pointing to the objects that are sitting on top of the desks.

'I'm not sure,' Lukas replies. 'They look like pictures I've seen of the first computers though.'

The objects have a large screen that is a deep blue colour and is set into a cream plastic casing. Underneath the screen is a flat metal box with a glass top. The entire arrangement is held up by a stand that looks like a giant foot.

'What do you think the glass bit is for?'

As I ask, I fiddle with it and see that the glass can, in fact, be lifted up. When I do so, the whole cartridge seems to slide forwards and it sits there looking at me like a wide mouth on a baby bird that needs feeding.

'I think you must put something in it,' says Lukas.

A quick look around reveals a very flat sheet of plastic on the desk next to us. I reach over and grab it, then hold it up in the light of the torch. The plastic is clear but there are regular, rectangular black patches all over it. I lower the torch.

'Hold it up again Lexi,' says Lukas. 'I think I saw something.'

When I do so, Lukas shines the torch directly behind it.

'Wow - look. It's tiny writing,' I say.

'Put it in the machine. It looks the right size to fit under the glass.'

I do as he says and push the glass cover back down.

This slides the capsule back under the screen.

'Now what?'

'Uhm... I guess it needs power if it's some kind of computer. Check the back of the machine.'

I feel around the back and my fingers brush a toggle-like switch, just to one side of the screen.

'Here goes,' I say, pressing it.

A bright light appears in the centre of the screen, gradually widening like a ripple spreading across a pond until the screen is all a hazy blue colour.

'Someone forgot to turn off the power when they locked this place up!' remarks Lukas.

But I am too captivated by the screen to think about this; as the blue light has spread, words have appeared. This time they are normal size.

'It's some kind of magnifying glass.'

'And that seems to be a list,' says Lukas.

'I think it must be a kind of catalogue. Let's work out how it's organised.'

I assess the rows and rows of names, titles, and reference numbers.

'There is a title here: "*Economics*". And below it are the names of authors and the titles of the books in that section. Each one has something called an ISBN number and finally a letter and number combination in the last column.'

'That must tell you what shelf it's stored on, don't you think?' Lukas suggests.

'Yes, but we don't want economics books. Shall we see if we can find any more of these plastic sheets? For other subjects.'

Leaving the desk and its glowing machine, we begin to walk around again. I see that the walls on the left hand side of the room are completely covered with cork tiles. And pinned onto them are old notices and some rather tattered looking newspaper front pages.

'Bank of England in Crisis,' I read out once I am close enough.

'Massive Fraud uncovered,' reads Lukas

'They must have been from before the Collapse,' I say.

'This looks like the last one,' says Lukas reading the sheet at the very end of the wall. The headline on that page is just a single word with a photograph underneath.

'Hope,' I read and I stare at the now familiar face of Nathaniel Jefferies.

I am trying to imagine what it must have been like back then, with the country in chaos, when Lukas points to the other side of the room.

'Lexi, look! Filing cabinets!'

The tall metal cabinets are similar to some I have seen in the school office and I press a small button at the side of one to unlock it. One by one we pull out the drawers and gaze at the thousands of plastic sheets that are neatly stored inside. Every now and again, between the sheets of plastic are pieces of stiff white card with writing on them. They stick up above the sheets.

'Particle Physics,' I read. 'Philosophy.'

'What shall we look for?'

'What about one of Ben's words that caused interference?'

'How about Darwin?'

'OK, let's look under 'D' and see if there are any books about him.'

It only takes us a few minutes to find it. Behind the card marked Darwin, there are dozens of pieces of plastic sheeting. We remove a couple and go back to the magnifying machine. Carefully placing the sheet in the mouth, I slide the capsule under the screen. In front of us appears a list of books, articles and papers.

'I suppose it's like a Flow search,' says Lukas. 'Just a bit slower!'

'I suppose it is,' I say, thinking about it. 'And you have to go and get the book off a shelf rather than clicking on a link.'

'But hopefully when you get there, there won't be bits missing,' adds Lukas.

I can only raise my eyebrows. 'Yes, let's hope.'

'Look at this one,' Lukas says. 'It's called *"On the Origin of Species, by Charles Darwin"*. That sounds good.'

'What's the shelf code?'

'Well, all the things on this sheet seem to be near one another actually - on various shelves of Rack F.'

'Come on then, let's go and find them.'

Chapter Fifteen

THE BEAGLE

Rack F turns out to be back the way we came and we heave the bookcases apart in order to expose the shelves that we are looking for. I shine the torch across them.

'This is an enormous section,' I say. 'Whoever this guy was, there was a lot written about him.'

'I know. I've been trying to remember something, anything, about that trip to London I told you about. I was only five but I do remember the way that my mother spoke about him. As if he was really important.'

'And yet we can't find a trace of him on the Flow now.'

'No, so come on. Let's find out why.'

I watch Lukas as he reaches up to a shelf just above his head.

'These look colourful. Shall we try them?'

'Why not? I think they're children's books. At least they'll be simple.'

'Yes, some of the others look a bit heavy going.'

I open *The Kids guide to Darwin and his Ideas* and start to look at the pictures.

'I'm going to try this - *The Voyage of the Beagle*,' says Lukas.

We both slide our backs down the bookcase to sit on the floor. Lukas wedges the torch between two books on the shelf behind our heads and we settle down to read. I can feel the warmth of his body next to me and its contrast to the cold floor makes me inch towards him. I am vaguely aware that our legs are touching but we both become so quickly engrossed in what we are reading that I do not move away.

'So this Charles Darwin character was a kind of explorer then?' Lukas asks after a while.

'I'm not sure. Perhaps more of a philosopher really.'

'This says he went on a five year voyage around the world on a ship called The Beagle.'

'Yes, but I think it was the ideas that he came up with when he got back that made him famous.'

We continue to read, both of us captivated by the material we have found.

'Lukas, listen to this; *'Darwin could find no other explanation that would account for everything he had seen. He concluded that the earth was in a constant state of change and the creatures on it were continually adapting to it.'*

'What does it mean?'

I read on.

'His idea was that over generations, an organism could gradually alter its features until it was in fact a new type of creature. It evolved into a new species.'

'But that's blasphemous.'

'It sure is.'

'How would he ever have got these ideas published?'

'I'm not sure. Maybe it's like the Party says; back then the churches weren't strong enough and people got away with more.'

'I suppose so. Does it give any more details of these ideas?'

'I don't know. I'll read on.'

Only a matter of minutes later, I can't stop myself interrupting Lukas once again.

'It gets worse.'

'Tell me.'

'It's not just creatures on the earth. It's us.'

'What do you mean?'

'He suggested that *people were not any different from other animals.'*

'What!'

'He thought we'd also evolved from some other creature.'

'Man did?'

'Yes, apparently he said *'light will be shed on the origins of man','* I say. 'But he definitely thought his theory explained where man came from. He was challenging the whole Creation story.'

141

'It's science fiction Lexi - all of it. This Darwin guy was clearly some crackpot. No wonder they took everything off the Flow.'

'You're probably right.'

'Shall we just go?'

I think for a moment.

'It *is* getting cold.'

'Come on then,' Lukas says and he moves a little in order to stand up. I feel the cold place on my thigh from his sudden absence.

'Actually,' I say. 'Let's stay a bit longer.'

He sits back down and smiles at me.

'Really?'

'Yes, Lukas listen, although I can see why the Party and the Sacellum wouldn't like Darwin's theory,' I say. 'It doesn't really explain why they ban us from knowing he ever existed. And look at all this... '

I sweep my arm across the expanse of shelves in front of me.

'That's an awful lot written about a crackpot. Maybe if we keep reading we'll discover something else.'

I can see Lukas looking at the rows of shelves in front of us, packed with books and other documents all on the subject of this Charles Darwin.

'OK,' he says eventually.

'Let's just read for another half an hour and then go,' I suggest.

Lukas answers me by picking up his book. I feel him edge closer to me again.

'Does your book show these birds' heads?' I ask,

showing Lukas a picture in my book when I get to one particular page about Darwin's voyage on the Beagle.

Lukas flicks through his book and shows me an identical page of sketches of finches. Some of the birds have huge strong heads and powerful, wide beaks and others are small with knife-like, sharp beaks.

'That's it,' I say.

'I wasn't sure I quite followed what he was saying about them.'

'As far as I understand it, Darwin suggested that they all started out from the same birds.'

'Yes?'

'And then some of their offspring were born with slightly different characteristics,' I continue. 'Which made them suited to living in a different place or to eating different food.'

'And over time they kept changing?'

'I think so...to make all the different types of finch that he saw.'

'And that was what became known as 'evolution'?'

I nod.

'Looking at them, they were well adapted to the different ways of living, weren't they?' I add

'Yes, but that's just the way the Creator made them. In the six days He took to make the world.'

'Oh, I know Lukas. I'm just trying to think why this idea might have caught on.'

We both go back to our books.

'It says here that he collected fossils on the Beagle trip,' says Lukas. 'That must be what I remember from my trip to that building.'

'Does it say what he thought they were?'

'Yes, apparently he thought they were the remains of creatures that had died out when they *didn't* adapt to change.'

I consider this idea and the fossils themselves for a few minutes.

'And yet the Sacellum insists they are made in Chinese factories,' I say.

'Yes, exactly. Although they can't have been... if he dug them up on is travels.'

'This just gets weirder and weirder Lukas.'

I continue to the end of the book and then place it on the ground at my side.

'It seems he was a religious man,' I say. 'To start with.'

'I think he studied theology at Cambridge.'

'But this trip of his made him question it all.'

'Well, there's questioning and then there's questioning!' Lukas replies. 'This theory that some organisms evolve from others because they are the most suited to survive, cannot in any way be matched up to the Sacellum's Creation story.'

'I know. And it's bothering me.'

'I'm sure other people have questioned the Creation story. You know how often we get warned about Scientia and their bizarre theories at school.'

'Mmm... but, as I said before, this is an awful lot of shelf space to be devoted to someone who was just stirring up a bit of trouble with a crazy idea.'

'True,' says Lukas and I watch as he flicks through his

book once more.

'Come on,' I say. 'I think we've given ourselves enough to think about for one night. Shall we go now?'

The two of us carefully replace the books and slide the shelf back into its original position. Our return trip along the passage back to the folly is totally different to the outward journey. Our sense of adventure and excitement has given way to heavier feelings. Rather than talk, I find myself falling behind Lukas to mull over what we found and almost before I know it, we are walking up the steps back into the folly.

'Wait here,' Lukas says as we reach the top step. 'Let me check if it's clear to go.'

From inside the stairwell, I see him leave the back door and then only moments later, stick his head back inside.

'All clear!' he calls in a loud whisper. 'It's dark over there.'

Together, we re-bolt the door and walk around to the front of the folly. I barely look at the Lodge as I tramp through the dew covered grass towards the door to the Warden's Garden and finally over the college wall and onto the street. Only once we are walking through the city do I feel like talking.

'Shall we go and see Ben and the others later?' I say.

'We should... and tell them what we found.'

'I wonder if they will make any sense of it?'

'I hope so. I'm struggling to,' says Lukas.

We walk the length of the High Street, the ancient university buildings towering on either side of us, and fall into an easy rhythm with our steps perfectly in time. It is nearly time for a change in prayer factions, so there are a few other people walking around and I hope that this will make us less obvious to any watchers. Even so, as we reach Magdalen Bridge, I move to walk just a little way in front of Lukas, to make it seem as if we are not together. Although the lights on the cameras are all red as we pass them, I am not willing to risk an over zealous fellow pedestrian deciding to report us to an Enforcer.

'It's nice out at night isn't it?' says Lukas after a while. 'Everything looks so clear in the moonlight. It's better when they don't have the lights too high.'

I stare at one of the streetlights ahead of us. It occurs to me that the illumination level hasn't been raised for months.

'It is. You know the Party mustn't think we're completely back to our old ways, despite what the Sacellum says... or they would have raised the lights.'

'True.'

We walk on, turning into the Iffley Road.

'Shall we go out again tonight?' Lukas asks suddenly.

I stop. We are in front of a community centre that used to be a Christian church. I move into the shadow of one of a dozen yew trees that are sprinkled across the lawn in front of it and turn to him.

'What do you mean? You mean go back to the library?'

He nods.

'Wouldn't you like to?'

I think for a few moments.

'I think I would,' I reply.

But then I see a change in his expression.

'What? Do you think we should we stop now? Not push our luck?' I ask, remembering the sight of Felix Cater standing in his window looking across at the Folly.

'No - it's not that.'

'What then?'

'Oh you're just not quite how I thought you'd be, that's all.'

'What do you mean?'

'Well you and Tish have this reputation at school'

'What kind of reputation?' I ask.

'Well, you know.'

'No, I don't know,' I say rather angrily. 'Tell me Lukas.'

'For only thinking about Screenings and shopping trips,' he blurts out rapidly.

I am speechless.

'They got you very wrong though, didn't they?' he says quickly. 'I always hoped that they might have.'

I feel a lump in my throat.

'Is that really what people think of me?'

Lukas blushes and looks flustered.

'But they don't know you Lexi do they? How can they when we are kept apart like we are?'

I shrug.

'Well, I don't care what they think anyway,' I say and I step back out onto the pavement and begin to walk. 'You'd better go Lukas. I need to get home.'

I am trying to get away from him, but he walks around in front of me, and as he passes, I see he is frowning.

'I will still see you at Ben's later though?' he asks.
'Won't I?'

'I expect so.'

'I'll be there about 5 - OK?'

'OK.'

I slow down and watch as he walks away, looking back just once over his shoulder.

Chapter Sixteen

THE ARREST

I am lying in bed trying to let sleep over-take me. My mother came home about an hour ago and peered around the doorway to check on me. I kept the covers drawn up over my head, but I guess the situation outside must be getting worse; she hasn't done that for years.

I imagine Lukas sitting with his prayer faction in the cold Sacellum. I hope he isn't too tired. And then I remember that I'll be there myself in a few hours and I must use this chance to get some rest.

But something about Mr. Darwin is bothering me.

I grab my earphones and switch my player on - Xentricity usually works on nights when I can't sleep. I try to relax. I think about lazy afternoons with Tish in her room, listening to tracks and eating popcorn. But then I recall Lukas' words.

'... you and Tish have this reputation at school; for only thinking about Screenings and shopping trips...'

When I wake, I am late. I grab a piece of bread, quickly put some jam on it and eat as I dress. Finally, pulling my robe from its hook and scribbling a good morning note to my mother, I am ready to leave.

'Lexi?'

Her voice sounds bleary from the first floor.

'Mum?'

'I wanted to catch you before you left?'

'I'm late mum. Can it wait?'

'Yes, I guess so. It's just... '

'What mum? I'm really, really late already.'

'OK, just... be careful won't you. There's going to be an announcement.'

'I'll be fine mum. Don't worry so much.'

She doesn't reply.

'See you,' I shout and I slam the door behind me.

It is nearly the end of my prayer session, and I am completely shattered now. I must have only had a couple of hours of sleep in the end but I still can't stop thinking about last night. Ben is leading my prayer group today and I keep wanting to pull him over to the side of the Sacellum and tell him all about the books in the Bodleian. Earlier on, I managed to tell him that Lukas and I would like to come round to his house at five. But time is going so slowly.

'Let us give our final prayers,' comes the instruction over the loudspeaker. It is just a recording of the Pastor's voice. They try to pretend that it isn't; that he is back there leading the worship. But Lukas told me that you can hear a crackle from the recording if you listen carefully and once I had picked it out, it is all that I can hear now.

'Forgive those who have succumbed to evil. Been led by temptation into the realms of the Underworld... '

I let the words drift over me as I kneel on the floor. I try to imagine what the churches must have said to Charles Darwin when he published his ideas. Last night in the library, I agreed with Lukas that he must have been some kind of crackpot to suggest what he did. But the more I think about it, the more I realise that he must have been pretty brave. I contemplate what it would be like to take on the Sacellum. To challenge the Pastor.

And I cannot imagine anyone ever doing it.

Leaving the Sacellum, I check my watch. I want to go to Ben's now and discuss all this with him and the others, if they are there. But it's still a bit early. It has turned into the most glorious spring day and I can feel a little warmth from the sun on my face that is helping to hold back my tiredness.

Under the tree by the gate to the Sacellum grounds, I spot a figure; a person, sitting on a bench, facing away from me. They have an aura of peace, almost a serenity that envelops them. Most people scuttle around like frantic worker bees these days; racing from Sacellum sessions to work and looking after family and the sick. It has all taken its toll on the everyday courtesies and kindnesses that used to see neighbours asking after one another or offering to look after each other's children. But this person seems strangely unaffected by it all, a throwback to a happier time. As I move closer, the shadow shifts and the glare of the sun reveals them to me. With a jolt, I see that it is Lukas.

In the instant that I recognise him, he turns, as if he has sensed me. And with embarrassment, I am forced to remember my sulking dismissal of him last night.

'Hi,' I say nervously. 'Are you waiting for *me*?'

'Of course,' he says, removing is earphones. 'Who do you think?'

'I told Ben,' I say, to change the subject. 'He's going home now... we could go over there in a few minutes.'

'Brilliant! I can't stop thinking about it. I couldn't sit at home, so I thought I'd come and escort you to his house myself.'

I laugh.

'How gallant you are Lukas Svoboda!'

He bows theatrically.

'Go up and I'll be there in a minute,' says Ben when we meet him outside his house. 'I just want to wash my face; I've been up for hours.'

'We won't stay long Ben,' I reply. 'We just wanted to tell you what happened.'

I follow Lukas through the house and up the ladder to the attic.

'There were another thirty people missing from my

faction this afternoon,' I say as I sit down.

'All sick?' he asks.

'I guess so.'

'My faction was twenty short. One of them was Frank Jenkins. You know... the sweet seller in the market? Apparently he died yesterday – he was only ill for twenty four hours.'

I feel as if I've been punched in the stomach.

'No... not Frank,' I whisper as tears fill my eyes.

Lukas reaches over and holds my hand.

'I'm so sorry Lexi. I forgot you would have known him.'

'It's not your fault. I can't stand this Lukas. Frank only ever helped people. He was so kind to my mother and I over the years. Why should he need punishing?'

'I don't know. The lady who lives opposite me lost her three-year-old boy a couple of days ago. She is wandering around like a ghost. She can't sleep. She can't eat. My mum keeps taking her food but she won't touch it. She just wants to be with her son.'

'Oh Lukas; that's terrible.'

'I know. I just wish it would stop. Surely we've made amends now?'

'You would have thought so.'

'What would you have thought?' Ben says from down in the bathroom. I see his head pop through the hatch.

'Oh... hi Ben. We were just talking about how many people are ill now.'

Ben's face drops.

'They say it's nearly a thousand with over four

153

hundred dead,' he tells us as he joins us on the beanbags. 'I just don't know what to say to anyone anymore.'

'I'm sure they're grateful for your help Ben.'

'I don't know. I feel useless,' says Ben. 'Anyway, come on you two, tell me what you found.'

I look at Lukas and grin. He nods at me to start.

'It was amazing Ben,' I say. 'We found the library!'

'The tunnel entrance was in the Folly,' Lukas adds.

'So Lukas was right.'

'Yes, we couldn't see it at first... '

'... but then we found an entrance at the back... '

'... and when we'd opened the door... '

'... we just walked down the steps... '

'... along this amazing carved out tunnel... '

'... through another huge wooden door and... '

'... there it was... the Bod... '

Ben is smiling and looking from Lukas to me and back again as we talk.

'What?' I ask

'Nothing,' he says. 'Carry on.'

'Can I tell him about the machines Lukas?'

'Go ahead.'

I describe the magnifying machines and how we had used them to find the shelves on which the information about Charles Darwin was kept.

'So who is this guy then,' asks Ben.

'Well, he was alive in the 1800s,' says Lukas. 'He wrote a famous book in 1859.'

'It was called *On the Origin of Species*,' I add.

'And did you find anything to explain why we can't

find him on the Flow now.'

Both Lukas and I laugh at this point.

'Did we ever,' Lukas says. 'You won't believe what he suggested.'

'Well?'

'He basically suggested man had gradually evolved into his current form from some kind of ape.'

Ben looks shocked.

'Well, more accurately, people took his ideas and got to that conclusion,' adds Lukas.

'But what about the Creation?'

'I know. We couldn't believe what we were reading,' Lukas says.

'What happened to him?' asks Ben.

I let Lukas explain because something has just occurred to me and I need to think it through.

'Apparently there was an enormous debate about it,' he says. 'He spent years trying to come to terms with the idea himself. But he felt he couldn't explain what he'd seen any other way. Although, he obviously upset everyone religious when he first suggested it.'

'And did they have him put to death?'

Lukas stops.

'Did they?' asks Ben.

'Uhm,' Lukas says. 'You know what. I don't think they did.'

They both look at me.

'No, in fact Ben... ' I say. 'I think he lived for years. There was a photograph of him as an old man in my book; he had a long white beard. I think it was the one I saw on the Flow.'

'From what we were reading, it's as if his ideas really caught on,' says Lukas. He is also now looking more perplexed.

'I think they called the idea 'evolution by natural selection',' I add.

'What about after he died?' asks Ben. 'Did you read anything about how they eventually dismissed the idea?'

'No, we didn't, did we Lukas?'

He shakes his head and now I understand what has been gnawing away at the back of my mind.

'You know what Ben,' I say. 'I'm not sure they did dismiss the ideas until quite recently.'

They both stare at me.

'What do you mean?' Ben asks.

'Well, think about it. Lukas remembers going somewhere in London where he saw some of the fossils Darwin used to back up his idea. So people must have still tolerated the idea then... to have had them on display. And there were huge numbers of books and papers and lots of research in the Bodleian all about the theory.'

'So do you think people still believed him right up to the Collapse?' Lukas asks. 'When the Party arrived?'

'It's possible isn't it?' I ask. 'It might explain why all information about him has been removed from the Flow. Perhaps it's all too recent for comfort.'

We consider this possibility.

'But why would they need to hide it from us once Nathaniel showed us that the theory was wrong?' asks Lukas.

'I don't know,' I say. 'You would think they would

use Darwin as a warning, wouldn't you?'

Ben suddenly stands up and begins to walk around the attic now. He is looking at the sheets of paper on the wall.

'The thing that bothers me most about all this is that it is more proof that we were right... about the memories.'

'It is?' I ask.

'Yes, look, if this Darwin guy wasn't discredited until the Collapse, then why can't I remember anything about him?'

He looks at us intently before answering his own question.

'Because something is stopping me.'

'We need to keep going,' Ben continues. 'We have to find out some more about what happened after Mr. Darwin proposed his idea.'

'What do you mean?'

'Well, if he proposed this in 1859 and the Optimas Party came to power over one hundred and fifty years later, what happened in between? I'm wondering if these other interference images could be anything to do with that. I'm convinced they are related.'

'We can check the rest of the material on the shelves,' I say. 'We're going back tonight.'

Before Ben can answer, there is a long ring on the front door bell. Even as he is climbing backwards down the ladder and walking across the bathroom floor, the ringing starts up again. And again as I hear him walk down the stairs.

And then there is just shouting and Ben's voice speaking loudly and insistently.

'Please. Calm down. I'm sure we can clear this up.'

Lukas and I look at all the paperwork scattered on the attic floorboards.

'We need to get out of here,' he says to me. 'If they come up here we'll be arrested as well.'

'Hold on Lukas. Perhaps we should just pull up the ladder and stay here?' I say.

'Do you think?'

'How would we explain having been upstairs in Ben's house together if we go down there?'

'You're right. Let's pull up the ladder, shut the trap door and hide.'

We try not to make too much noise as we lift the rickety loft ladder. Once it is up, Lukas leans over the edge of the hatch and reaches for the trap door to pull it up into place.

'Careful,' I say, holding onto his legs to stop him tipping forwards.

Finally, we are sitting, both crouched down, arms folded tightly around our knees, just to one side of the hatch. Only then do we stop to listen to the continuing noise from downstairs. We have switched off the light so we can only just see one another in the faint glow from the bathroom.

'How many of them do you think there are?' I whisper.

'It only sounds like a few.'

'Can you think of anything we could say to them to explain this?' I say, sweeping my arm across in front of us.

'No - we're in big trouble if they find us,' he says. 'But perhaps Ben can hold them off long enough. If they take him away now, then perhaps there will be time to get out of here before they come back for a search.'

'I should have listened to my mum,' I say. 'She was trying to tell me something this morning.'

'What about?'

'I don't know. I didn't give her chance to explain. She seemed worried... said there'd been an announcement. I just thought she was worrying about nothing like usua...'

'Shhhh... '

We hear footsteps on the stairs. Coming up towards us... into the bathroom. Someone reaches up and grabs hold of the catch for the loft. This is it.

Light floods into the attic from below and a shaggy head of hair is visible in the hole.

'What are you two doing in the dark?' says Ben's voice.

'Ben?' I cry.

'Yes, who did you think it was?'

'They haven't taken you away?' I say. But then I have another thought. 'Are they still waiting downstairs?'

'Josh and Krish are downstairs,' Ben says. 'But something terrible has happened and you two need to get out of here.'

'What's happened Ben?' I ask.

'They've arrested Carrie,' he says.

Chapter Seventeen

THE DOUBLE HELIX

'Go on, go!' says Ben. 'Get out of here you two. I don't know how long we have and I need to hide these papers.'

'No, Ben - I'll help,' I say. 'This isn't just your problem.'

'Me too,' agrees Lukas.

Ben doesn't argue.

'What's the plan?' I ask.

'I don't know. Hide it all I guess; under the floorboards or something.'

'Hold on. Remember the Party worker in Reading - they tore his house to pieces when they searched it,'

Lukas reminds him.

'Yes, we need to get everything out of here,' I say. 'Put it somewhere else... where they won't think of looking.'

'We could take some to my dad's factory?' suggests Lukas.

Ben looks at him and I can see he is considering the suggestion. But then he shakes his head.

'No. That's too dangerous. I don't want to get anyone else involved.'

'But I'm already involved,' says Lukas.

'Yes, but you've only been coming here for a week or so. The cameras have hardly been switched on at all in that time - thankfully.'

'So you think the Enforcers won't link us to you yet?' I ask.

'I'm hoping not. Josh, Carrie, Krish and I will appear on their recordings. But we're all Sacellum workers. We can probably make up some reason for getting together.'

'But you couldn't explain us,' I add.

'Exactly! We need to keep you two out of it.'

The three of us begin to put all the papers in piles and pull the large sheets down off the roof rafters. I start to roll them up.

'I have another idea,' says Lukas suddenly. 'But it's incredibly risky.'

'Go on,' says Ben.

'Take everything to the Sacellum.'

'You're kidding!' I exclaim.

But Ben just looks at Lukas and then smiles.

'Brilliant. They'll never think of looking there.'

'I guess so,' I say, rather unconvinced.

'But the problem is going to be getting everything there and hidden without people seeing,' says Ben. 'And doing it before the Enforcers come and search here.'

We are all silent for a few seconds.

'How about we gradually take it up there - in prayer sessions,' I suggest.

'But we need it out of here now,' Lukas reminds me.

'I know,' I say. 'But we could take it to my house now. And then I could gradually bring it to the Sacellum.'

'It'll be dangerous Lexi... ' Ben says. '... but I guess it might work.'

'It will Ben - think about it. I live so close that we can get everything out of here in about fifteen minutes if we get a move on. And as you said, they have no reason to suspect me. And then I can get it up to the Sacellum over the next week or so.'

Ben doesn't take long to decide.

'Come on then. There are some old packing boxes over there from when I moved in. Let's get this stuff packed up and over to your house.'

It takes only a few minutes to clear up everything in the attic. Lukas goes down to tell Josh and Krish the plan, whilst Ben and I start emptying the packing boxes of Ben's old clothes and filling them with the research materials. When Josh returns with Lukas, he is like a caged animal in the confined space of the loft, pacing back and forth and barely helping us at all.

'What happened?' I ask him. 'To Carrie?'

'It was the new regulations,' says Josh.

'What regulations?' I ask.

'The quarantine,' he replies.

'What's that?' asks Lukas.

'They made an announcement earlier,' says Ben. 'Someone has suggested that no one be allowed to enter or leave Oxford. I got a message on my tablet when I got back from prayers.'

'What? When was this?' I ask.

'Today... earlier,' says Josh. 'Carrie was trying to get back home to Banbury. She was sure they wouldn't catch her if she just went back quickly. She wanted to get some of our old Flow search results; ones that first showed how much the facts were changing.'

'And they arrested her on her way home?' Lukas asks.

'For breaking the quarantine,' Josh says.

'But the trouble is,' adds Ben. 'We actually think they may have got her when she was trying to get back into Oxford - with the papers.'

'It won't take them long to do a facial recognition search of the reconnaissance tapes,' says Krish who has joined us all now. 'They'll see how often she's been coming here and they'll come after me, Josh and Ben next.'

'I'm not sure the papers will be enough on their own to get her sentenced for treason,' says Ben. 'But they'll definitely do some investigating.'

From the attic, we move the boxes to a pile just inside Ben's front door.

'I'll go out and see if the camera is on,' I say.

'If they're on Lexi, then just go home. Don't come back here. It will look too suspicious. We'll come up with an alternative plan for the papers,' says Ben.

'OK,' I agree reluctantly.

But when I emerge from Ben's house I cannot help but grin to myself; it's red. If they did find papers on Carrie, they haven't traced her to Ben's house yet.

I spin on my heels to make it seem to an observer as if I've just forgotten to tell Ben something, and push open the front door.

'All clear,' I announce triumphantly.

In my brief absence Lukas has come up with an idea for getting the boxes to my house without arousing suspicion from our neighbours.

'We're going to put the boxes with some bags of old clothes in a wheelbarrow and make it look like we're doing a charity clothes collection,' says Ben. 'We'll go to the whole street and knock on their doors to see if they've got anything.'

'But when we get to your house, we'll actually remove the bottom boxes and leave them there before we carry on,' says Lukas.

It works a treat. We are given some bags of clothing by every house between Ben's and ours. Then when we reach my house, Lukas steadily passes the boxes of papers across the threshold to Ben while I grab one or two pieces of old clothing from my cupboard to give them in return. When we are done, Lukas and I remain behind while the other three continue up the street. It takes us no more than two or three minutes and I'm pretty sure that even a particularly sharp-eyed observer would hardly notice what's happened.

'Ben told me to leave some of the papers in the collection box when I go into the Sacellum each day,' I tell Lukas as I shut the door and we turn to look at the pile in our front hall. 'It's his job to empty it apparently.'

'And where's he going to put them when he's got them out?'

'He said he would find somewhere - that it would be better if we didn't know.'

'OK, do it carefully though, won't you Lexi? Make sure it's not obvious you're up to something.'

'Of course. Come on, let's get these up to my room. I have a cupboard in there where they will be safe for a few days.'

Once the boxes are safely hidden, I shut the cupboard door and turn around to talk to Lukas. He has sat down on my bed and suddenly swings his legs up onto my duvet and leans back against my pillow.

'So, who do you have pinned up here then?' he says, looking at the posters above him 'Of course - Xentricity! I should've guessed.'

'Why don't you like them?' I ask.

'It's not that I don't like them,' he replies, 'But like I told you, concerts aren't my thing - too painful.'

'Oh yes - I forgot you heard the sounds at concerts too. How has it been recently?'

'Pretty bad actually; terrible in the Sacellum. I'm wearing earplugs every day now.'

I'm about to ask Lukas whether he really thinks

someone could be purposefully using these sounds to disrupt our memories, when I hear my front door open.

'Lexi,' comes my mother's voice from the hallway.

'Oh no! Lukas stay here; she'll go crazy if she finds you up here. I'll be back in a minute.'

I leave before he can reply and when I am downstairs, I follow my mother into the kitchen.

'Hi mum,' I say breezily.

'Hi Lexi,' she says and looks at me a little strangely. 'Everything OK?'

I realise I had been uncharacteristically cheerful with my greeting.

'Fine... what've you been doing?' I ask more sullenly.

I watch as she starts to potter around the kitchen.

'Working at the Mosque. We've been getting it ready to take patients. The Cathedral is full.'

'It's not getting any better then?'

'No, not at all. And from my basic tally I reckon one in three is dying now. It's just horrific Lexi. You're still feeling OK?'

'Fine. So all this prayer isn't helping then?'

She shakes her head.

'Why not mum?'

'I don't know Lexi. I'm terrified we're missing a trick. Something we could be doing to help.'

'What do you mean?'

'I'm not sure sweetheart - don't take too much notice of me. I did get the Sacellum to set up a quarantine area though.'

A heavy weight feels as if it has plummeted into the

pit of my stomach.

'What?' I ask.

'They've put a security cordon around Oxford to prevent people leaving or entering the City.'

'The quarantine was your idea?'

She nods.

'I thought it might limit the sickness.'

'But I thought we were sick because people are sinning again - turning their back on the Creator?'

'Yes, that's what the Pastor says.'

'So how would a quarantine area help?'

'Well, the Pastor agrees it will keep temptation and evil out of the City while we try to mend our ways.'

As I sit looking at her, all I can think of is Carrie sitting in an Enforcer cell.

'I hadn't realised it was your idea,' I say.

'Hmm... well, I just hope it will help. We've got to do something.'

Feeling a little stunned by this unexpected development, I get up. I remember Lukas lying on my bed.

'I've got some schoolwork to do mum. Are you in prayers soon?'

'Any minute.'

'I'll say goodbye now then. See you later.'

'See you later sweetheart.'

When I return to my bedroom, Lukas is still lying on my bed. His eyes are closed and I see the slow rising and falling of his chest; he has fallen asleep.

I stare at him and I think how peaceful he seems and

for a few minutes I just stand inside the threshold and examine his face. His dark hair is splayed out on my pillow and his lips are gently parted. His face is smooth; I'm not sure he's even started to shave. And yet, I remember angrily, he is about to be paired for life.

I am brought back to the present by the click as my mother shuts our front door behind her. The sound also disturbs Lukas who opens his eyes and I can see him taking a few seconds to remember where he is.

'Hi,' he says a little blearily. 'Sorry - I didn't realise how tired I was.'

'It's not a problem,' I say.

Now that I am looking at Lukas with his eager face and awkward smile, I cannot bring myself to tell him about the quarantine and the fact that it was my mother who thought of it. He might think badly of me.

'I thought we were going to the Bodleian?' I say instead.

'Still want to?'

'Of course.'

'Well, we'd better get going then.'

Heading into Oxford along the Iffley Road, we see the first obvious signs of the quarantine. There are yellow cloaks everywhere and although we live inside the cordon, one glance up the road out of town reveals a new checkpoint, only a few hundred yards further out towards the ring road.

'We need to walk separately,' says Lukas as soon as he sees the situation.

I mutter my agreement and allow him to stride ahead

of me.

As Lukas pulls away, I am aware of a scuffle behind me and natural curiosity makes me turn to see what is happening. A man, probably in his thirties, is fighting against a group of Enforcers. His purple cloak is billowing around his head as he is kicked and punched to the ground. As we watch, a dark coloured saloon car screeches to a halt beside them and the man is bundled inside, still shouting and lashing out at his captors. And then, as fast as it seemed to start, it is over. The car speeds away, and the dozen or so observers in the street are left staring at the space that it briefly occupied.

'Move along now people,' comes a voice. 'Move along. Nothing to see here.'

One of the Enforcers is speaking into a megaphone and I turn quickly to obey his instructions before he can make eye contact with me. In doing so, I see that Lukas had also stopped to watch. I am pretty sure that he too is thinking about what we are about to do and what these officials would make of it if they knew.

We both keep our heads down for the rest of the journey. Although it is still before curfew, there is almost no one on the streets. I feel acutely aware of how unusual a young girl on her own must look to any casual observer. But if I move too close to Lukas then this will give rise to even more suspicion. By the time we reach the gates to Dartford College, just as the sun is setting, my nerves are more rattled than I was expecting.

'That was worse than last night,' I say. 'I can't believe that walking through town could be more scary than walking on the towpath!'

'There's certainly a different feel in the air,' agrees Lukas. 'Come on, let's get inside before someone spots us out here.'

The two of us scale the wall just like before and drop down on the other side. But this time we discover that we are not alone in the College gardens. Off to our left, at the edge of the quad that makes up the first courtyard, there are two men in uniform. And one of them has a huge dog with him. They are carrying flashlights and sweeping them in wide circles as they walk. Instantly we see them, we crawl to the base of the wall and hide behind a row of tall bushes.

'Who are they?' Lukas whispers.

'No idea,' I reply. 'Although they're wearing the same uniform as Peters sometimes wears so I'd say they could be college security staff.'

'Good thing we didn't get here a few minutes ago.'

'Yes, I think we just missed them. Let's go as soon as they go into the next quad.'

From behind the foliage we watch the men continue on their patrol. Although I'm wary of them, it is the dog that bothers me most. It looks restless and edgy and pulls constantly on its lead. Then just as they are about to leave through a narrow passageway, it suddenly stops and turns. It begins to growl and bark ferociously. The handler turns too and has to lean back to counterbalance the force of the dog as it lunges forward.

'Hey calm down boy! Calm down. What've you seen, eh?'

Beside me I hear Lukas take a sharp intake of breath

and we watch the two torch beams criss-cross the expanse of grass between us and the two men. Finding no one on the lawn, they begin to investigate the borders; exploring dark corners behind trees or large shrubs with their powerful lights. They are working slowly, methodically, along the first, second, third side and now we see the beam hit the wall against which we are pressed.

Slowly the light gets closer and closer. The dog is still straining on its lead. We curl ourselves up as tightly as we can and pull the branches of the shrubbery across our faces.

A dismembered voice echoes loudly through the darkness.

'Come in patrol two. Come in.'

I feel my body lurch. Beside me I hear Lukas make a tiny involuntary groan.

But then we see one of the men fumble for something attached to his belt. He speaks into a small handheld receiver.

'Roger Gate house. Patrol two here.'

'We need you at the main gate boys. Got a bit of a situation here. Copy?'

'Copy that Fred. On our way,' says the man and he disappears through the passageway, followed by the dog handler who is having to drag the agitated animal behind him.

For a moment neither Lukas nor I can speak. Eventually he stirs us back into activity.

'Come on Lexi,' he says. 'Right now, we'd be safer in

that tunnel than we are out here. Let's go.'

'Coming,' I say and we make our way to the Warden's garden.

Thankfully, Felix Canter is not in his study this time and so, skirting our way around to the back of the folly, we can quickly re-enter the tunnel and make our way into the underground bookstore.

Once we are sat in front of one of the magnifying machines we take a few minutes to recover from our nerve-wracking journey.

'OK - what are we searching for today?' Lukas asks eventually.

'Well, we decided with Ben that we needed to find out what happened once Mr. Darwin proposed his idea, didn't we?'

'Yup.'

'And I remember that there was a book on the shelf next to the one I had last time. I think it might be useful.'

I take the torch and go back to Rack F returning a few minutes later to sit next to Lukas at the little desk.

'Here - *"What did Darwin ever do for us?"*,' I read from the front cover.

I flick through the first few pages and we see the same information that we discovered last night. There is a picture of the ship, The Beagle, on which Darwin made his five-year voyage. There is a cartoon of him as an ape. But then the information about Darwin himself seems to end.

On the next page is a picture of a monk in a habit. He is shown next to some diagrams showing pea plants of various sizes and the pea plants that had grown from their seeds.

'What's this about?' Lukas asks.

'The caption says - Gregor Mendel used the physical characteristics of peas to demonstrate his ideas on inheritance.'

'Inheritance!' repeats Lukas.

'Yes?'

It only takes me a few seconds to remember.

'The word from Josh's search!'

'And look,' Lukas says pointing to the diagram below the sketch of the man. 'The family tree thing that Josh saw in the interference image.'

He moves the book across in front of himself to read the title of the diagram.

'A pedigree showing the inheritance of short and tall peas in Mendel's breeding experiments.'

We read the paragraph of text alongside.

'So he bred a tall plant with a short one but only ever got short or tall ones from the seeds. Never middle sized ones,' says Lukas.

'Yes, I think that's it,' I say. 'And he concluded that there must be some method by which the characteristics were being passed down to subsequent generations. Some means of inheritance.'

'Some offspring got one version of a kind of instruction and grew tall and others got the other version and stayed short.'

'And it says here that if characteristics can be inherited, then a new characteristic that gives one individual an advantage can be passed on and could lead to permanent evolution of the way the organism looks or behaves.'

'Darwin's idea,' Lukas says.

We look at the diagrams and sketches for a few minutes.

'So 'inheritance' *was* linked to 'Darwin',' I say. 'Ben was right. The interference images are linked.'

'Shall we keep going?' says Lukas.

I turn the page and read the title.

'Chromosomes, Genes and DNA.'

This time at the top of the page is a photograph. It shows two men, one either side of a complicated metal structure made of clamps and pieces of wire and balls of plastic. They are looking at it intently.

'Watson and Crick with their double helix model,' I read from the caption beneath.

I put the book between us and we start to read the text.

'So now people were trying to find out how characteristics were inherited,' I say to Lukas at the end of the first paragraph.

'Yes, they seem to have thought they found a chemical in the body that would do it.'

I read on.

'This DNA thing... in something called a chromosome?'

'It's so complicated!' says Lukas. 'My brain is hurting with all these new words.'

'I know. But all these people Lukas... working for all this time on these things...all based on Darwin's theories. Doesn't it make you think.'

'And us having never even heard of Darwin,' he adds.
'It's...unbelievable.'

I stop reading and flip the page over.

'Lukas!'

'What?'

'Look,' I say and I point to a diagram on the middle of the next page. It shows two coloured strands weaving their way around one another up the page in an open twisting spiral. And between the two strands are horizontal lines... like the rungs of a ladder.

'It can't be,' I say.

'What?'

'My mother's bracelet.'

'What do you mean?'

'My mother has a gold and silver bracelet which looks exactly like that, and she never takes it off.'

Chapter Eighteen

THE ALCHEMIST

'Are you sure it's the same?' Lukas asks

'Definitely. The bracelet has two twisted strands of gold and then silver rungs between them. Just like these bits here,' I say pointing to the picture. 'It's such an unusual arrangement - I know it's the same.'

'Where did she get it from?'

'That's always been a bit of a mystery Lukas. She's never given me a straight answer,' I say quietly.

'Well, it says here that this is the structure of the chemical that people thought somehow controlled what features a living thing had. This is the 'DNA' it mentioned on that last page.'

'What else does it say?' I ask, too confused to keep reading.

'The molecule was able to copy itself and be passed down from one generation to another,' Lukas reads. 'It contained a kind of code or set of instructions that defined the organism's appearance.'

'The inheritance that that monk had seen,' I mutter.

'But scientists also discovered that the code on the molecule could occasionally go wrong,' Lukas continues. 'It says this was known as a mutation.'

'What happened then?'

'Uhm, hold on. Well, sometimes the organism would die. But apparently sometimes the mutation made it stronger or better able to survive.'

'Darwin again,' I point out. 'Lukas, you know, this is all getting too weird.'

'I know. All these bizarre words and ideas.'

'Yes, but what I really mean is that this is a whole world of theories seem to be linked together and which were obviously so important not very long ago.'

'Yes?'

'And yet I keep coming back to the fact that we know nothing about them. No one out there knows about this stuff. Even though it seems to be about the history of the world and the creatures on it.'

Lukas sits back in his chair and the two of us stare at the blank screen on the magnifying machine in front of us. All these new ideas are ricocheting around in my head. And now I have the added issue of my mother's bracelet.

'What's on the last page?' I ask eventually, since we

have nearly finished the book. 'Perhaps this is where we find out it was all proved wrong; how the Creator showed us we'd been mistaken.'

Lukas turns the page.

'Genetics and advances in medicine and health,' he reads from the top of the page. 'Doesn't look like it.'

We both read this final page.

'So people manipulated this code... tinkered with it and altered it,' I say.

'This must be why we don't know about it,' says Lukas.

'Is this what caused the Collapse, do you think?' I ask. 'The Creator was so angry about people doing this stuff that he sent Nathaniel Jefferies to show us the error of our ways.'

'The Pastor does says that people thought they didn't need to believe in a Creator,' Lukas adds. 'This must have been what he meant.'

I look at the pictures on this last page.

'I guess so. It is terrible to think that people could have really believed all this was possible with our own hands. And yet...'

'What?'

'Well, most of these things would seem like good things to have done,' I say, pointing at the pictures. 'They were able to produce new organs for people who were dying, they made crops that could feed twice as many people or which were full of extra vitamins and they made medicine that cured people of all sorts of illnesses.'

Neither of us speaks for a while.

'But think about it Lexi. It must be why none of this is on the Flow now,' says Lukas. 'The Collapse came along and everyone realised that we had become too arrogant and abandoned the Creator - and suffered as a result.'

'I don't know Lukas,' I say. 'There's still something that's not right about all this.'

'Let's look up something else from Ben's list then - just to make sure.'

'OK,' I say and I absent-mindedly flick through the book in front of us. It falls open on the page showing the twisting DNA molecule and I think of my mother.

'Virus!' I say suddenly. 'The word my mother used that was on Ben's list.'

'Right,' says Lukas and he puts his hand around the back of the magnifying machine in front of us in order to switch it on. I push back my chair and go across to the filing cabinets to search the plastic sheets under 'V'.

'Here... a section on viruses. A dozen or so sheets,' I say, turning back to Lukas who is sitting staring ahead, a ghostly blue shine on his face from the warmed up screen.

We slide in the sheet and up comes the list of items.

'Mostly in Rack R,' I say. 'Come on. It's down there.'

We move along the shelves, searching for the labels and when we find Rack R, we push hard to roll it away from its neighbours. Shining the torch across the expanse of papers and books in front of us, I pick a book at random.

'"*Computer Security and Common Software Viruses,*" by J.S. Peters,' I read from the cover. 'This just looks like something you would get on the Flow now.'

We walk along the length of Rack R, pulling out various other publications. But they all seem to be similar. Full of symbols and special notations and names that I have seen flash up on my tablet when my security software is running through a document.

'I guess 'virus' was just an error then,' says Lukas when we get to the end of the shelf. 'Any more you want to look...'

He stops. All the lights in the underground room have suddenly come on. We can also hear faint voices.

'Quick Lukas... hide!'

'Where?'

'Good question.'

There is nothing here except rows of bookcases. But Rack R has an empty shelf at the bottom. It must be about half a metre high and the shelves are about the same depth. I reckon it would just be big enough. Glancing across to the opposite shelf that faces it in Rack S, I see an equivalent, slightly longer shelf that is also missing its contents.

'Down there?' I say, pointing. 'We could lie flat on the shelves. At least we'd be out of sight.'

Lukas looks skeptical.

'Where else Lukas?' I whisper sharply. 'If they don't actually walk down here, they *might* not see us.'

'OK, let's do it,' he says. 'I can't think of a better plan.'

We lie down and both manoeuvre into position like pupating caterpillars. When we have finished, my head is resting on two books that have fallen flat at the end of a row and Lukas has squeezed himself in across the way with his knees folded up to cram them into the available space.

'Where do we find these papers then?' says a voice from over to my right. It is a powerful, commanding voice and I recognise it all too well.

Felix Canter.

My legs begin to shake. I close my eyes and try to wish myself somewhere else.

'Over here sir,' comes a quieter voice. 'We can use these machines to find what we're looking for.'

'Get on with it man. Vaccination - I want to see everything you have on it.'

'Of course sir. Just a second... oh... that's strange.'

'What?'

'One of these screens appears to be switched on.'

'What do you mean?' asks Felix Canter and I hear a loud scraping sound that I think must be a couple of desks being pushed roughly aside. 'How can that be?'

'I'm not sure sir. I can only assume...'

'What?' Felix Canter yells impatiently.

'... that someone else has been here looking at these catalogues before us.'

'How could they?' comes the booming reply. 'This place is supposed to be sealed up.'

I look across at Lukas. He is lying still, his eyes closed but I see that his mouth is moving. No sound comes from his lips but I guess he is praying. I'm not sure prayers are going to be any use to us if Felix Canter finds us here.

'Yes, sir...' I hear the second man say, followed by a single word. 'Viruses?'

I assume he is reading from the screen.

'Why would someone need to look up about computer code?' he continues. 'It's all on the Flow.'

'It doesn't matter what they were looking at,' Felix Canter says sharply. 'I want to know how anyone can have got in here at all.'

I wriggle in close to the back of the shelf on which I am lying; willing myself smaller and smaller.

'Could they still be here?' he suddenly asks. 'Where are these books on viruses they were looking at?'

'Rack R sir. This way.'

I hear their feet come rapidly along the corridor at the side of the bookcases. I imagine them checking down each one as they pass.

'Here sir... R.'

There is silence for what seems like an age.

'What's this?' I hear Felix Canter say.

I wait for a hand to pull me out of my hiding place and I attempt to draw myself even tighter into the back of the shelf. There is a long pause.

'Perhaps someone left it years ago sir,' says the other man.

'Maybe... well it doesn't seem as if anyone is here now. But tell me Mr. Jones. How could anyone have got into these rooms?'

'I don't know sir. The door from the Flow reading rooms is always in plain sight. One of the staff would have seen if they had entered the same way as we did.'

'So how did they do it then?'

I can hear he is getting more impatient now.

'Well, there is the tunnel sir,' suggests the man. 'From the college... the Gladstone Tunnel.'

'A tunnel?'

'From the folly sir. In the Warden's Garden sir.'

'There is a tunnel?' Felix Canter repeats again.

'Yes sir, but I don't think anyone would remember that it even exists anymore.'

'And where does this tunnel bring you in?' says Felix Canter, ignoring the man's comments.

'Down there sir.'

I hear them walking away; towards the wooden door that we had used earlier.

'Lock it,' says Felix Canter 'Do you have a key?'

'Yes sir... on the wall there.'

No more than a few seconds later, I hear the heavy thud as the man shoots the bolt across inside the lock.

'I think I'll keep this key and post someone in the Folly. Just in case they think of coming back again,' says Felix Canter. 'And I want to know if any of your staff have seen anything.'

'Very good sir,' the man replies. 'Shall we look for those papers now?'

I hear a pause.

'No - I'll come back tomorrow for the papers. I need to sort this out now. We cannot have anyone, ANYONE, coming down here.'

'No, sir.'

'I personally persuaded the Party to leave these books here. They cannot be the cause of any trouble. Understand?'

'Yes, sir.'

The voices gradually recede and once everything is silent, the lights go out as suddenly as they had come on. I give myself a few seconds to calm down.

'You OK Lukas?' I say eventually.

'Yeh - you?'

I roll out into the corridor and fold my legs up under me so that I am sitting on my knees and shins. I look at him, still prostrate in his hiding place.

'What did he say he wanted to look up? - did he say *vaccinations*?' I say.

'I think so.'

'But the Pastor says vaccinations are the work of the devil,' I say.

'He does.'

'Shall we go and find out what it says about them down here then? See if it's different from what the Pastor says.'

'No, Lexi, that was too close. Let's just go.'

'Really?'

'That man is going to be my father in law. I can't be found down here. You said yourself how frightening he is.'

'I know. But there's got to be some reason he couldn't find what he wants on the Flow. Why he came down here.'

'I guess so.'

'Please let's just see what we can find.'

'I don't know.'

'Five minutes... that's all. You heard him. He's gone to sort out putting a guard in the folly. He's coming back tomorrow. This will be our last chance to look at anything down here. He'll make sure it's completely secure now.'

'Exactly! Shouldn't we go out before he puts the guard at the folly?'

'No, because we can't go that way anymore anyway,' I say. 'They've locked the wooden door haven't they?'

'So how are we going to get out then?'

I pause.

'We'll have to go out via the Flow reading rooms. The way they came in. Which means it's an even better idea to wait a while before we leave.'

'But the man says that's watched all day.'

'But not all night.'

'What do you mean?'

'We could go out that way in a few minutes. Then we could find somewhere to hide in the reading rooms until they open and just walk out like one of the normal Flow readers when the reading rooms open in the morning.'

I finish triumphantly and he visibly sags.

'OK Lexi - you win. Although it sounds too simple.'

I shrug.

'Do you have a better idea?'

Lukas shakes his head.

'So we can just quickly look at the information on vaccinations then?' I ask.

'OK,' he says.

There are a few books on vaccination, but most of the items on the shelf are leather bound compilations of various monthly magazines.

'The Journal of Vaccination and Vaccines,' I read from a wrinkled spine. 'These look like very specialist articles.'

'Specialist newspapers for alchemists and stargazers. Look at this stuff Lexi - the Pastor would make a giant bonfire out of all of it.'

'Which makes me wonder even more what Felix Canter wants with them.'

I take out one volume of papers. Inside the front cover is a list of the contents.

'Global epidemiology of Meningococcal disease,' I read.

'Come on Lexi. Let's go. This won't ever mean anything to us.'

But just as I am about to agree, I see something that stops me cold.

'No. Lukas, I can't.'

'Why now?' he says, sounding frustrated.

'Look,' I say putting my finger underneath one of the titles.

'Antibody recognition of Avian Flu protein and possible implications for a universal vaccine,' he reads aloud.

'Not the title... the authors.'

'J.P.Franks, F.L.Levy and J. Z. Drachmann?'

'Yes - J. Z Drachmann,' I repeat. 'He was my father Lukas.'

For a moment he is silent.

'Your father was an alchemist?' he eventually asks.

'My mother never calls him that,' I reply. 'But other than his name, she's never told me much else.'

Chapter Nineteen

THE PACT OF OBEDIENCE

'I have to keep this,' I say and I tear at the front page in the binder.

'Lexi, no; if they find you with that, you'll be flogged to within an inch of your life... or worse. This isn't some book of herbal remedies like the Mansours had.'

'No, I know. But I've got to find out what my father has to do with this. Why does Felix Canter want to know about the thing that my father worked on? About vaccinations?'

'But look at this stuff; how can you hope to understand it?'

I stare at the words on the page in my hands. I barely

understand a single one. I cast my eyes along a shelf of books above the journals.

'Here... I'll take this as well then... a simple text book,' I say, grabbing at a thin booklet and stuffing the torn page into its cover.

'But if they catch you... '

'I'm just going to take that risk,' I say. 'I don't expect you to understand Lukas. You have a mother and a father that you see every day. You don't know what it is like to grow up with so many questions. And my mother... '

'OK, OK,' Lukas says and he gently puts his arm around me to calm me down. I slump against him.

'I'm sorry. I can't explain it... but I have to have this book. I have to find out more.'

We stand together for a few minutes, the adrenalin rush from the sight of my father's name has now passed and I am suddenly exhausted. Lukas gently steps away from me but still holds both my hands.

'Come on,' he says and he pulls me towards the other end of the room. 'We're going now.'

I allow him to steer me past row after row of bookcases and finally up a set of winding stairs.

'Who knows how long it will be until someone comes to open up the Flow rooms in the morning,' he says as we reach a door. 'We need to find somewhere comfortable to wait.'

Lukas gently pushes against the door. It moves a little. He puts his eyes to the strip of light coming in from the other side and then opens it further to stick his head out.

Finally he pushes it fully open and we both walk through and into the Flow reading rooms of the Bodleian.

Light from the street lamps outside is flooding in through the windows and we creep around, looking for somewhere to spend the next few hours in safety. Just near the main entrance, we find a room. It isn't locked. Boxes of paper are stacked on the floor and several shelves and cupboards store other printing materials: consumables for the printers that are lined up along one wall outside. There is plenty of room for two people to crouch down behind the containers and we are near enough to the door to make a run for it as soon as we are able in the morning.

'This'll do,' Lukas says and he clears a space on the floor just big enough for the two of us.

'I've just realised that I'm going to miss my prayer faction in the Sacellum,' Lukas says once we are sitting down.

'Oh no Lukas - I hadn't thought.'

'I don't suppose it will matter. Perhaps they'll think I'm sick.'

'But then your name will go on the list.'

'Oh well.'

'But then everyone will say you're a sinner and you know you aren't?'

'Aren't I?'

'What do you mean?'

'Think about it Lexi. What would they say if they could see us here?'

I think about that for a moment or two.

'But we aren't doing anything wrong?'

'Aren't we?' he says. 'Anyway, it doesn't matter because that isn't what would be said if anyone saw us, is it?'

I don't want to think about this. Sitting here with Lukas doesn't feel wrong.

'None of it is making any sense to me any more,' I say.

'I know what you mean,' he replies.

We turn so that our backs are against one another.

'Try to get some sleep,' Lukas says.

'What if your name goes on the list and Felix Canter calls off the wedding,' I ask when the thought suddenly occurs to me a few minutes later. 'Your parents will never get over the shame.'

'No... ' says Lukas, '... but perhaps it wouldn't be such a bad thing.'

'The shame?'

'No,' he laughs. 'Calling off the wedding.'

'Lukas!' I say. 'How could it be a good thing? You're so lucky to get Tish.'

'That's what my friends say.'

'But you don't agree?'

'Oh... I don't know... I'm just not sure Tish and I are very well suited... that's all.'

'They must have thought you were Lukas - the people who organised the allocation. Why don't you?'

'Uhm... it's hard to explain really. I know it must seem pretty crazy to you. She's your friend. But we just sit and look at each other when I visit. We've nothing to say.'

I think about this; Tish and I can talk for hours.

'Give it time,' I say. 'She's so nice Lukas. You'll see in the end.'

'Maybe,' Lukas says and after a long pause he adds, 'Thanks. We should get some rest.'

I close my eyes. Lukas' body is supporting mine and waves of sleepiness begin to waft across me. My eyes are heavy and as I am falling asleep, I think about what he has told me. I can't imagine him finding it difficult to know what to say to anyone.

I'm woken by the rattle of keys.

I nudge Lukas and quickly put a finger to his lips to keep him from speaking. We can hear a worker moving around the room outside, pressing switches and gently singing. One by one the lights come on above our heads and the gentle hum of Flow terminals gets ever louder as they are all fired up ready for the day.

I lift up a single finger and mouth the word 'one'. Lukas nods his head. We can hear the person moving around at the far end of the Flow reading room now, so we move to the door. Lukas opens it slightly. I am trying to make some hand signals to suggest that we go, when I hear a loud metallic thump followed by something hitting the ground. I jump.

'Post,' whispers Lukas with a smile.

I smile back and, with rapid signalling and nodding of heads, we agree that we should go before the worker returns to collect it.

So I hold my book on vaccination tightly in my left

hand, under my cloak and sprint after Lukas. He gets to the door and yanks it. Unexpectedly, a little bell rings.

'Come in - I'll be with you in a minute,' comes a voice from the room next door. 'Sit where you want.'

But we are gone.

Lukas is walking ahead of me now and I am trying not to look as if we have ever met. But as we walk along the High Street, I become aware of a yellow shape in the corner of my eye.

'Over to the left,' I say in a loud whisper and I see Lukas turn his head ever so slightly.

'I'll just keep walking,' he mutters. 'You stop. I'll see you later.'

Doing as he suggests, I turn to look in a shop window and see my reflection. Behind me, I also see the Enforcer with his tablet raised. I tell myself to stay calm. He can't have seen anything. He lowers it. Probably just testing me.

I slowly set off again, remembering the boxes of Ben's papers in my cupboard. I keep my left hand wrapped tightly around the book under my cloak.

Finally, once I am on the road out of town, I allow myself to speed up and am almost jogging when I reach the top of my road. But then I stop.

In front of me are six yellow figures.

As they move around, their cloaks flutter like butterfly wings in a summer breeze. But this is just an illusion of tranquility, for as I approach my front garden, I hear that they are shouting aggressively at one another and at someone in the house.

'Pull up the boards in the loft,' one of them calls to a colleague who is leaning out of an upstairs window. 'And get that chimney breast checked in the kitchen.'

I do not look at them. I try not to think what they are doing to the house - and to Ben, wherever he is. I just put my hand on the latch of our gate and I walk up our path, looking straight ahead of me.

'Lexi?'

My mother runs towards me the second I am in the door.

'Where have you been?' she says hugging me.

'What's going on?'

'They've taken that Sacellum worker away - you know, Brother Benedict. The one that came to talk to you the other evening.'

'Why?'

'I don't know. They don't tell you, do they? But where have you been?'

'I just went out for a walk.'

'But you've been gone hours. I thought you were in trouble.'

'I need to talk to you mum.'

'What's happened Lexi? Is it to do with that Benedict?'

'No. Well, not really. Look mum I need some answers.'

'What do you mean?'

'I need you to tell me the truth.'

'About what Lexi?'

I pull my cloak up over my head and reveal the book

beneath.

'Can we go and sit down? I need to ask you about this.'

My mother looks at me in horror.

'What's that?'

'A book.'

'What kind of book? Why were you hiding it?'

I ignore her questions and walk into the kitchen. I pull out two chairs and sit down on one.

'Mum, what did dad do?'

She takes my cue and sinks down into the other chair.

'I have told you before that I will not discuss your father,' she says firmly and looks at me with a steely determination in her eyes.

'Did he give you the bracelet?' I ask.

Her hand goes to its outline under her sleeve.

'What? Why?'

'Because I've seen a picture of something that it is modeled on. Something called DNA.'

She looks confused for a minute.

'What? Where did you hear that?'

'Never mind that... is that what it is based on?'

'I don't know what it is based on Lexi.'

I look at her. She has a genuinely puzzled look in her eyes. Seeing it finally confirms for me, what Ben had been so convinced of earlier. Someone must be using the memory disruption on us all. But even if she can't remember what he did, there are other questions that she could answer.

'Mum, please. I know something is going on. I heard the Pastor say something to you about a deal that you did. Something about dad.'

My mother starts to open her mouth but I'm not going to be fobbed off this time.

'I know you can't tell me much about him. But there must be something. Was he an alchemist like they say?'

She is silent. I can still hear the distant sounds of the Enforcers stripping out Ben's house. I wait. Eventually, she speaks.

'I don't like that word Lexi. They call him a sorcerer...an alchemist... when they talk about him. But I think he was a scientist. I'm sure there was a difference.'

I nod.

'All I know is that they arrested him. Shortly after they came to power, the Optimas Party declared that the sorcerers were responsible for many of society's problems. They rounded them up.'

'So he's not dead then?'

'I don't think so.'

'Where did they take him?'

'I don't know.'

'Can't we find out?'

'No.'

'Why not? I want to see him.'

'We can't. That was the deal.'

'The deal? The one the Pastor mentioned?'

She pauses.

'Yes,' she says quietly. 'The Pastor says your father made a deal with them. He would stay out of trouble if they left us alone.'

'What do you mean?'

'And they made me agree to be obedient, or...'

'Or what?'

'Or they would take you away.'

We sit looking at one another.

'It's why I'm always so careful Lexi. They would have taken you away.'

I think about what she is telling me and about our lives.

'But what was it that dad did that was so bad?' I ask eventually.

She stares at me.

'Tell me mum,' I shout.

'I'm not sure I ever knew exactly,' my mother replies. 'I know the Party said he was working on something very dangerous and he had to be stopped.'

'But did it have something to do with the bracelet?' I ask.

'Yes, I think it may have. I'm pretty sure your father gave it to me shortly before he was taken. And I've never seen anything like it since.'

Chapter Twenty

THE FIFTH COMMANDMENT

A week later, as I walk up the road on my way to the Sacellum, I see Mr. White's big black hearse drawing up, almost silently, outside Mrs. Novak's house. I bow my head and stand still as six burly men go into the house and then reappear carrying the wooden casket on their shoulders. I had heard her husband was ill but I didn't know he'd died. Poor Mrs. Novak. She's always been so friendly to us even though my mother is divorced. Through the front window I see her tiny hunched figure staring blankly out at me. I smile, but she turns away; a tall, young man tenderly putting his arm around her from behind and steering her into the depths of the house. It could have been the son she always used to talk about. Seeing him reminds me that it was only a few weeks ago that I noticed her enthusiastically congratulating Lukas on his allocation to Tish. And now she is burying her own husband; alongside so many others in the new burial ground out on Portmeadow.

'Lexi?'

I turn around when I hear the familiar voice.

'Ben!'

'How...'

'They let me home last night.'

'Oh, Ben. I'm so pleased. What happened?'

'Well, they still have Carrie. They don't accept her explanation for the papers but they couldn't find any evidence against me or any more against her.'

'We were so worried.'

'Thanks but I'm OK. I'm pretty sure they'll be watching me closely for a while though.'

'The cameras have been green since they took you.'

'We'll have to meet in the Sacellum from now on.'

'You think it'll be safe to talk there?'

'Yes, safe enough. Anyway, tell me how you've been whilst I was gone.'

'I'm OK. I'm not ill, if that's what you mean.'

'That's a relief. Is your mum OK?'

'Yes, I really worry about her working with all the sick people but she tells me she'll be fine.'

'I'll pray for her Lexi. She's helped so many people.'

'Do you think it will be over soon Ben?'

'I don't know. I hope so.'

We both turn and walk up the road, various members

of my faction appearing from side roads as we continue.

'But tell me what you've been up to when you've not been at the Sacellum,' he says.

'We went back,' I reply in a whisper.

'To the library?'

I nod.

'But Felix Canter arrived too - whilst we were there.'

'He didn't catch you?'

I shake my head.

'It was close though. He knew someone had been there and I don't think we'll get back in again.'

'Did you find anything else useful?'

'I don't know where to start Ben.'

'About Mr. Darwin?'

'Well, yes, but mostly stuff that happened after he died.'

'Like?'

'Uhm... well, it seems that his idea was taken seriously... Lots of other work was done and slowly people worked out an explanation for how organisms could change over time. Like he proposed.'

'What kind of work?'

'A monk did experiments with pea plants. He showed characteristics could be inherited by offspring from parents.'

'Inheritance!'

'Exactly - Josh's flow search.'

'And?'

'And they eventually thought they had found some kind of chemical that would carry this information inside of us. People worked out what it must look like and how it could copy itself.'

'And how did this fit with Darwin's idea?'

'Well, they proposed this thing called a mutation - if I've understood properly.'

'A mutation?'

'Yes, they thought that sometimes this 'code' got altered and the result was a slightly different organism or feature.'

'OK,' Ben says slowly but I can see he is as confused by these ideas as I am.

'It's complicated but I think the idea was that this change might make the creature better or stronger or quicker or more able to climb a tree or something like that. And so it could adapt to new environments or survive better if its environment changed.'

'Mr. Darwin's idea,' says Ben.

I nod.

'Wow. So the interference images were definitely linked.'

'Yes.'

'Did you check them all?'

'Not quite - Felix Canter interrupted us.'

'But we have enough to know it's no accident. That these things are missing from the Flow for a reason.'

'Yes... and there's something else Ben?'

'What?'

'I found my father's name on some papers down there.'

'Your father?'

'We went to see what Felix Canter had been so interested in. He was looking for information about vaccinations. And my father's name was there.'

'Hold on a minute... vaccinations?'

'Exactly,' I say. 'How many times have vaccinations been given as an example of the arrogance of alchemists. It must be the Pastor's favourite sermon.'

'So why would Felix Canter be researching them now?' asks Ben.

'I don't know. I took a book to learn a bit more about how they were meant to work. I've been reading it at home.'

A flash of concern passes across Ben's face. As he speaks, his left arm moves across his body and he cradles his right elbow gently.

'Be careful Lexi. You don't want them taking you in for questions.'

I can hear the warning in his voice and I examine his face more intently. His cloak hood is pulled up tightly around his neck and face but just spreading out under his chin I see a yellowish green mark; a bruise spreading like an inkblot across parchment.

'I am being careful. I promise. But I have to know what my father was working on and also why his name was there,' I say. 'I asked my mother but all she said was that the Party thought he was a danger to society.'

'So what did you learn... from the books,' he asks.

'Er... well, the booklet basically ran through the history of vaccinations - starting in 1796 with the first one used against smallpox.'

'1796! That's over two hundred years ago!'

'Yes, I know. It seems that they weren't just some modern invention used by alchemists to deceive the population like the Pastor always says they were.'

'So how were they supposed to work, these vaccinations?'

'They are injected into your arm and they just kind of made your body fight the little organisms that were making you ill.'

Ben appears to consider this for a minute.

'Wow, so, your father? How was he involved?'

'Well, the journal we found said he was working on a vaccine for an Avian Flu.'

'Flu?'

'Yes, but I can't work out what this means because I thought 'flu' was just a high fever.'

'So did I.'

'It seems they wanted to use a vaccination instead of just asking the Creator for forgiveness.'

'Perhaps people didn't understood that these fevers were sent by the Creator,' Ben suggests.

'Maybe,' I reply.

'And you said your mother doesn't know anything about it?'

'No, she just said dad had been arrested for his work. She made a pact with the Party about him. She promised to be obedient so she could keep me,' I say.

Ben is quiet for a moment.

'That explains it.'

'What Ben - explains what?'

'Your mother.'

I stop walking.

'What about her?'

'You don't know?'

'What?'

'She was famous Lexi. She was the most amazing mathematician. The Party used her to create the trading algorithms. The ones that rescued the economy.'

'You're kidding. You must have made a mistake Ben.'

'I haven't.'

'But she's just my mum. She's a market trader who does maths tricks in her head. Who obeys every rule the Party and the Sacellum ever sent her way as if her life depended on it.'

'She is now. But after the Collapse, she worked for them. And then she turned up here. No one could understand what had happened.'

We have reached the Sacellum door now and I go to take my place in stunned silence.

I am still thinking about this new revelation as I leave the Sacellum. My father first and now my mother. Neither of them appears to be the people that I thought they were. I stride out for home, oblivious to the exhausted worshippers around me and only when I am nearly there do I take any notice of the insistent voice behind me.

'Lexi... Will you stop for a minute...? Lexi!'

I turn.

'Lukas!'

'What's the matter with you?' he asks. 'I was shouting and shouting.'

'Sorry, I was miles away.'

'I couldn't get over to see you - it wasn't that I didn't want to.'

'Don't worry Lukas. I understand; we need to be careful. I didn't expect to see you again straight away.'

'OK. As long as you're not mad,' he says. 'I just thought after Felix Canter nearly catching us... '

'Lukas - it's fine!' I say. 'I've been so pre-occupied with thinking about everything we found down there. Anyway... what are you doing here now?'

'I came to see Mrs. Novak.'

'Oh yes. I'm sorry. Did you know her husband well?'

'He was one of my dad's foremen a few years back... before he retired.'

'It's sad. She's a nice lady.'

'Yes, but what's the matter with you then? If you weren't ignoring me, what were you thinking about?'

I don't answer immediately.

'Lexi?'

'Lukas, are you busy?'

'I do have to go and see Tish in about half an hour?'

'OK, never mind then.'

'No, come on. Can you walk with me?'

'I guess so.'

'Right, I'll get my bike.'

'I've found out a bit more about these vaccinations that Felix Canter was so interested in,' I say as we walk.

'And?'

'Everyone really did used to think they could stop us getting ill.'

'That would be good right now.'

'Exactly! That's just what I was thinking.'

'So what are they?'

'It seems that people thought you could have something injected into your body and it would know how to fight certain 'bugs' that could make you ill.'

'Bugs?' asks Lukas. 'The Pastor says it's sin.'

'I know he does Lukas. But I'd say if Felix Canter is down in the Bodleian library researching vaccinations, then he may not agree with the Pastor. Wouldn't you?'

'I see what you mean.'

'It seems that my father worked on them in some way. But all my mother can tell me about the work is that her bracelet probably had something to do with it.'

'The DNA one.'

I nod my head.

'What can the DNA have to do with vaccines?' he asks.

'That's the bit that I'm trying to understand.'

The two of us are just on the edge of town and I look around me to see where the nearest cameras are. Lukas and I have been careful to walk the required distance apart all the way. But what I am about to do may arouse suspicion if it is clearly visible to an Enforcer.

I look for cameras and see the monument in the middle of The Plain. It is a circular stone gothic tower, about five metres high. But it is hollowed out inside and along the inside walls are stone benches.

'Come on,' I say to Lukas and I begin to cross the road towards it.

'Where're you going?' he says, jogging to catch me up.

'Inside,' I reply, ducking my head to avoid hitting the stone archway that makes the entrance.

Lukas sits down opposite me.

'What's that?' he asks, looking at the paper that I am pulling out from under my cloak.

'The introduction to that paper that my dad wrote. I was studying it inside my prayer book in the Sacellum.'

Lukas looks around him in a panic.

'Calm down,' I say. 'I checked the cameras. None can see us in here.'

He checks outside and seems to conclude that I'm right.

'I don't know what's happened to you?' he says, shaking his head.

'I'm not sure I do either,' I say truthfully. 'I'm not the person that I thought I was at all these days.'

'So what does it say? The paper?'

'It seems that my father was working on a vaccine that he thought would stop people getting ill from something called Avian Flu.'

'People sometimes say 'flu' now when people have a high fever don't they?'

'Yes, but I've never heard of Avian Flu.'

'I remember something called Spanish Flu.'

'You do?' I ask hopefully. 'What was it?'

'I don't know. I just remember hearing the words when I was young. Millions of people died from it I think.'

'Well, this paper is about fifteen years old and it talks as if this Avian Flu was very dangerous too,' I say. 'And it seems to suggest people were worried that it would change to become even more deadly.'

'How could it do that?'

'That's what I'm trying to figure out. The paper is ripped where I tore it out. Look,' I say and I hold it out for him to see.

Lukas reads aloud from the page

'The authors have set out to determine by genetic sequencing if there are regions of the Avian flu vir... identical across all strains of the pathogen. Regions which define functions that are essential to the survival... and which therefore will be present in all active strains. Any mutati... d occur in the future which would make the virus more deadly ...eater threat to the world population would have to occur outside these regions in ord... to retain its ability to survive. This could provide an opportu...ersal vaccine to be developed i.e. one that would be poten... possible future Avian Flu types.'

'Do you understand any of this?' he says.

'Not really. I was trying to think of possibilities for some of the gaps while we were praying.'

'And did you get anywhere?'

'Maybe.'

'Go on then.'

'Well, the first thing I noticed was this Lukas,' I say and I point to the word in the third sentence.

'Virus!' he says. 'It's the word we looked up in the Bodleian!'

'Exactly. But this has got nothing to do with tablet code. There must be another meaning that we didn't find in the library; a separate section or something. And back then everyone obviously thought that these kind of viruses made people ill. So that means one of the words in the first gap is probably 'virus' too. Here.'

'So something like *'The authors have set out to determine by genetic sequencing if there are regions of the Avian flu virUS THAT ARE identical across all strains of the pathogen'*?' Lukas suggests.

'Yes.'

'But what does it mean?'

'I'm not sure?' I say. 'This word 'genetic' was in that book on what Darwin did for us. They used it when they were talking about the DNA stuff.'

'So they are talking about that code maybe?'

'Yes, perhaps they were looking for sections of the code that were the same.'

'Any more?'

'Well, the next sentence reads, *'Regions which define functions that are essential to the survival... something, something, something... and which therefore will be present in all active strains.'* There it doesn't seem to matter much what's missing. I think these strains that they talk about are different versions of the thing that was making people ill.'

'And they were looking for a section of code that was present in all of the different versions because it was 'essential'.'

I nod

'But I was stuck on the third sentence,' I say. 'I feel I should know the word, like its on the tip of my tongue but I can't quite place it.'

'Any... something... occurring in the future which would make the virus more deadly... something... eater threat to the world population would have to occur outside these regions in... something... to retain its ability

to survive,' Lukas reads.

'Yes. So they are talking about something which would make this virus more deadly and threaten everyone in the world.'

'And the thing would have to happen outside some region.'

'The region they were talking about at the beginning?' I suggest. 'The region of the code?'

'A mutation!' says Lukas suddenly. 'Remember? What it said in that book? Mutations were when the code had gone wrong. It would fit.'

'So... a mutation could make the virus more deadly... and threaten everyone,' I say.

'But... it couldn't be in the essential region... because if it was...then the virus would die,' Lukas finishes for me.

'Thank you Lukas - that must be it.'

I lower the paper and stare out across the traffic and towards the University buildings in the centre of town.

'So your dad was working on some virus that people thought would threaten the world. Here in Oxford,' says Lukas.

'So it would seem,' I say. 'And my mum was right; it did have something to do with the bracelet. Look at this last sentence.'

'This could provide an... it must say something like 'opportunity'... *vaccine to be developed i.e. one that would...* 'work on?'... *possible future Avian Flu types,'* reads Lukas.

'He was looking for sections of the DNA that they could use to make a vaccine. Sections that wouldn't change even if the virus had one of these mutations that made it more deadly.'

'And this was all to do with something called Avian Flu.'

I fold up the paper and put it in a pocket of the jeans I am wearing beneath my cloak. I stand up and step back out onto the road. Lukas follows and we begin to walk towards Dartford College again.

'So back then people thought that high fevers... '

'Flu.'

'Yes, flu, could be cured by these vaccines,' I say. 'And some of these flus were given special names.'

'Like Spanish Flu and Avian Flu.'

'But then Nathaniel brought us the Book of Commandments,' I say, trying to fit this new information together with the facts as I've always been taught them.

'He taught us that prayer was the only cure,' added Lukas. 'That the fever was sent as a warning about how our souls would feel if they were sent to burn in the Underworld forever.'

'And so all the people who worked on all this stuff... hundreds of years worth of theories and ideas and discoveries... were just shown to be wrong,' I say.

'And they were locked up if they were still alive,' added Lukas. 'As blasphemers.'

I nod and we walk on in silence.

'But in that case Lukas,' I ask eventually. 'Why is Felix Canter trying to find information about vaccination at exactly a time when lots and lots of people are dying from a sickness that gives you a terrible fever?'

'And when we've been praying for weeks and yet only more and more people are dying,' he says.

The imposing entrance to Dartford College looms up ahead now and I slow down, turning to face Lukas.

'Do you think my father found a vaccine that he thought would cure people?'

'I don't know what to think.'

'Might that be why he was so dangerous that they had to lock him up?'

'It would make him a very dangerous person to have walking around if he really could make people better without ever stepping into a Sacellum.'

'But if he believed he could cure people then he was truly an enemy of the state. *No one but the Creator has the power to decide who will live or die.*'

'The fifth commandment,' says Lukas.

'Yes. Perhaps he truly did deserve to be detained?'

Lukas reaches for my arm but then appears to think better of it out here in the open.

'I don't know Lexi. But I have to go now. I'm late already.'

'Of course.'

'Let's talk about it later. Can you meet me down on Portmeadow after lunch? I am going down to pay my respects to Mr. Novak.'

'Isn't it a bit public?'

'No, it's quiet down there. There are no cameras because until recently no-one ever went there.'

Before I can reply, we hear a voice coming from

behind the small door that is set in the enormous College entrance gates and that is slightly open.

'What are you two discussing so avidly? I saw you from my bedroom window.'

I feel a slight fluttering in my stomach as I wonder how long she was watching us.

'Oh nothing important Tish,' I say and I quickly step forward to embrace the figure now stepping over the threshold.

'Laetitia,' says Lukas formally. 'You look lovely today. Are you well?'

I am taken aback by his formality and also surprised to see the annoyance in Tish's usually easy-going eyes.

'I'm fine. You're late,' she says to him.

'I'm sorry,' he replies. 'I got held up at a funeral.'

Momentarily she looks wrong footed, but quickly recovers.

'Of course. Sorry. Come in,' she says. 'Please come too Lexi. I haven't seen you for ages and I'm sure Lukas won't mind sharing me for once.'

'I'd be delighted,' Lukas says quickly.

As I follow her into the grounds and across to the door of the Master's Lodge I replay her words to Lukas. Something is familiar about them.

And then I have it. It wasn't the words; it was the delivery.

Tish spoke to Lukas exactly like her father speaks to her mother.

And what surprises me most is that Lukas already has the same tone of resignation in his responses as her mother.

Chapter Twenty-One

THE WARNING

'How've you been?' Tish asks me as we walk through the front door of the Lodge. She has linked arms with me and her deep amber eyes are filled with genuine concern. 'Are you better now?'

For a moment this throws me - until I remember that the last time she saw me, I was in the grips of my fake illness.

'Oh yes,' I say. 'It was really weird. When I got home, I felt so much better.'

'Dad said you didn't appear on the Pastor's list the following day.'

'No, it wasn't the sickness.'

'I told him you couldn't have been ill like everyone else,' she said. 'He said that it was sometimes impossible to tell everything about a person... But I knew you were OK.'

I contemplate Felix Canter saying that about me. I've never had much to do with him. And yet he seems to have formed an impression of me. I wonder whether that has anything to do with who my parents are. Now that I know about them, it occurs to me that it has been a miracle that he allowed me to be so close to his precious daughter for all these years.

'I'm sure your dad was just worried about you,' I say.

'Yes, you're right there. He's gone totally over the top.'

'What do you mean?'

'Oh... security. He's gone mad about it. There are guards all over college making sure sinners don't come anywhere near the Lodge. He was shouting about some old tunnel that he's discovered. It leads right into the grounds from town apparently.'

'A tunnel?' I ask, careful not to catch Lukas' eye.

'Yes, it's in the Warden's garden. Someone told him about it. But when he went to have a look for it, he found the entrance was already open. He's got this idea that someone was going to use it to break into the Lodge.'

As she lets go of my arm, I can't resist stealing a glance at Lukas.

'Did they find anyone?' he asks, ignoring me.

'No, but there's a guard out there all the time now.'

We follow her into the Canters' sitting room. It feels

weird to be here in the more formal surroundings when we're usually upstairs relaxing; discussing fashion or music in her bedroom.

'Mrs. Peters said she would leave us something to eat,' says Tish, once we are inside. 'Help yourselves.'

I see an enormous plateful of cakes and biscuits on an oak dresser at one side of the room. There is a jug of freshly made lemonade alongside with two plates and two glasses on a silver tray.

'Thanks Tish. I'm starving,' I say, walking over to it.

'I don't want any,' she says. 'You can use my plate Lexi.'

Lukas hands me a plate and then we both reach for a huge chocolate cupcake in the centre of the display.

'Sorry - you have it,' he says, laughing.

'Let's split it,' I say and pick up the knife to cut it in two.

'Hurry up you two,' says Tish from behind us. 'It's only cake.'

When I turn around, I see that she has sat herself down on an old Chesterfield sofa. Seeing me looking, she pats the space next to her.

'You can sit there Lukas,' she says pointing to a wing backed armchair on the other side of an ornate marble fireplace.

'Did you see the new recording on the Flow?' she asks me once I am installed beside her. 'I sent you the link yesterday.'

'Not yet, sorry Tish,' I say. 'I did see your message but I've been really busy.'

Her face collapses into a disappointed pout.

'I wanted to watch it in one go Tish. I was going to make some time tonight,' I say to cheer her up.

'Which band was it?' asks Lukas through a mouthful of cake.

'The Chills... you probably don't know them,' she tells him, before turning straight back to me. 'It's so great Lex. They've done this really funny video to go with the track. It's set in the Houses of Parliament and the band is jumping all over the benches where the politicians usually sit. It's called Freedom. How cool is that?'

'How on earth did they manage to film it there?' I ask.

'Dad sorted it out for them,' she replies. 'He had a call from their agent and he thought it sounded like a good idea.'

'I don't think my dad would know who The Chills were,' says Lukas.

Tish turns once more to face him.

'No? Well, my dad does,' she replies.

'It's still pretty amazing that he let them film in the Chamber,' I say quickly.

'He reckons if it gets people interested in government, then it's good for the country. Or something like that!'

'You'll be meeting them next,' I say. 'Take me with you when you do, won't you?'

'Only if you promise me that you'll watch the clip I sent you,' she says.

'Of course I will.'

'Send it across to me as well will you Laetitia?' Lukas asks her.

'You want to see it?' she asks. 'Really?'

'Why not?' he says. '...if it's so good. I do like music

you know.'

'OK then,' she says. 'I just hadn't thought it was your kind of thing that's all... but I'll send it later.'

'Thanks. I'd like that.'

I look from Tish to Lukas and back again. I think my presence is making things worse.

'I'd better go,' I say. 'I'm taking up your time together and I really should get home and see if my mum has any more news about this quarantine.'

'Do you have to go?' Tish says, grabbing my arm and holding me in my seat. 'I haven't got anyone to talk to - stuck here all day. I miss you.'

'And I miss you too Tish but I'm in the Sacellum again later and I really need to talk to my mum. You can talk to Lukas.'

'I guess,' she says. 'But if you must go, promise you'll come back and see me tomorrow... or the next day at least.'

'I will.'

'And you WILL watch the Flow clip?'

'Yes!'

I stand up to leave but before I can take a step towards the door, Tish suddenly shouts.

'Oh no! Stay there! You can't go yet; I forgot, I have something for you from my father.'

'You do?' I say. 'For me?'

'Yes. He made me promise to give it to you next time I saw you.'

'OK,' I say with a smile, although I am feeling anything but happy inside.

'I'll just get it,' she says and she leaves Lukas and I

alone in the sitting room.

'What is it?' I ask him in a fierce whisper as I sit down again.

'How should I know?' he hisses back.

Tish returns with an envelope. I look at her face; she looks her usual calm and immaculate self. I stand up as she walks towards me.

'What is it?' I ask, taking it from her.

'No idea,' she replies as she crosses the room and holds out her arms to Lukas. He seems to take an uncomfortable extra couple of seconds to understand that she wants him to hold her hands and I see him watching me out of the corner of his eye while he grasps her outstretched fingers.

I open the envelope, feeling physically sick as I do so. And when I see what is inside, my knees almost give way.

'Are you OK?'

After a few seconds confusion, I realise it is Lukas that is asking. 'You don't look so well again.'

I turn to face them both, my eyes processing the scene; the two of them, joined together as they will be for the rest of their lives. All of a sudden, my vision feels as fragile as my legs and their image swims in front of me for a second or two.

'I'm fine,' I say in a strangled voice. 'Fine.'

'You don't look it Lexi,' says Tish and she comes towards me now, discarding Lukas's hands like someone throwing stones into the bottom of a deep well.

'Perhaps I will just sit down for a bit,' I say. 'I must've

stood up too fast.'

I sit and put my head down low. I need to compose myself quickly. Before she calls for some help.

'There,' I say to my feet. 'Feeling better already. Sorry about that.'

I lift my head and concentrate on producing a smile that will convince them.

'Are you sure?' Tish asks.

'Yes, I'm sure. I'm just tired. Everyone's tired Tish,' I snap.

As soon as the words are out of my mouth I regret them. I hadn't meant to remind her that she's different. She can't help it if her father won't let her go to the Sacellum with everyone else. But then I study her face and realise she hasn't taken it the wrong way at all. She doesn't have any idea what I'm talking about.

'I'm going to go home for a rest,' I add.

'Lukas,' she says. 'You should take her home. Make sure she is OK. Yes?'

'Happy to.'

'Good. We can have our meeting another time. Can't we?'

'Of course, anytime,' he says. 'Come on Lexi. I'll walk you home.'

The instant that we are outside, I have to stop and lean against the college wall. I close my eyes.

'Lukas - he knows,' I say.

'What? Who?'

'Felix Canter,' I say. 'He knows it was me in the Bodleian book store.'

'How can he know? He didn't see us.'

'No... but I dropped this,' I say and I remove the envelope from my pocket and pull out the Significance Bracelet that is coiled up inside.

'A Significance Bracelet?'

'Yes, I noticed I had lost it a few days ago.'

'But how does he know it's yours?'

'Look at the thread.'

'It just looks like a regular Significance Bracelet to me.'

'Well, it's not. Tish gave it to me.'

'Oh...'

'Yes, it's a really expensive gold thread that she used to make it. The closest thing to a fancy piece of jewellery that I'll ever own.'

'And he knows that?'

'Yes, he bought her the thread and he knows she gave it to me on my thirteenth birthday.'

'And you're sure you dropped it in the library?'

'Not a hundred percent, but I noticed it was missing just after we got back from our last visit. I've been looking everywhere and I had begun to wonder.'

'Perhaps he found it somewhere else?'

'I don't think so. Look at the note that it was wrapped in,' I say and hand him a sheet of headed paper from inside the envelope.

'*Do not get involved in things you do not understand,*' Lukas reads. 'You're right; he knows.'

'But why hasn't he had me arrested then?'

'I don't know.... Perhaps because you are Tish's friend?'

'Maybe,' I say. 'But what do I do?'

'Stop investigating,' Lukas suggests. 'Heed his warning.'

'I suppose I should,' I say.

'Yes, you should Lexi. You really, really should. Let Ben and the others take it from here.'

'But...'

'No 'buts', Lexi. For whatever reason, Felix Canter is giving you another chance. Don't throw it away.'

Sharing the details of Felix Canter's threat with Lukas seems to have helped to calm me down. I move away from the wall and start to walk away from Dartford College.

'Come on,' I say. 'Do you still want to go down and pay your respects to Mr. Novak?'

'Yes, but are you up to it?'

'I'll be fine. Let's go.'

We head for the centre of town and shortly after leaving the college, I see the entrance to the Flow Reading rooms at the Bodleian and I remember our night spent in the printer room. As we turn onto the High Street, we meet a line of vehicles moving slowly in the direction of the burial grounds on Portmeadow. They are all carrying coffins. We bow our heads as they pass us and then join the funeral parade marching slowly in their wake. The silence gives me time to think.

Lukas and I separate ourselves from the crowd once we have arrived at the wide expanse of flood plain that is now the home to row upon row of brown mounds of mud, each with a small plaque at one end. Whilst the mourners continue with their ceremonies to our right, we make our way to the other end of the field, scanning the names on the graves as we pass them. When he is almost at the end of a row, Lukas halts abruptly and I see him drop to his knees and close his eyes. I crouch down beside him and rest my hand on his arm.

Once Lukas has finished his prayer, he sits on the damp grass between Mr. Novak's grave and its neighbour. I join him.

'Lukas I don't know if I want to stop investigating,' I say quietly.

'Tell me you are kidding,' he replies angrily

'No. Don't get mad,' I say. 'It's my dad, Lukas. I want to find out some more about him.'

'I know, but it's too dangerous Lexi.'

'But if I'm careful?'

'We thought we were being careful before.'

'Yes, but we won't have to go back to the book room.'

'So what are you thinking of doing then?'

'I don't know. But my dad was working on something that Felix Canter is suddenly really interested in.'

'I know but... '

'What if he did find a vaccine Lukas?' I ask. 'And what if the sickness everyone has at the moment is this Flu?'

He doesn't reply.

'If we could find out what my father discovered then we might be able to help people.'

'Lexi. Careful. The fifth commandment... remember?'

'I know Lukas. I'm not saying prayer won't be needed as well. But perhaps this vaccine thing will stop so many people dying.'

'But how would we find out more about your father's work without going to the book room?'

'I was thinking about that,' I say. 'He must have done his work up at the hospital. Don't you think?'

'The Radcliffe? I guess so. But it's pretty much all closed up now.'

'But we might be able to find some trace of what they did,' I suggest. 'Isn't it worth going to see if there is still anything there?'

'I don't know Lexi. That place must be crawling with cameras.'

'I was wondering if we could ask Krish... '

'Ask him what exactly?'

'Well... about the cameras; which ones are working. That kind of thing,' I say. 'Perhaps he can find us some information on the Flow about the layout as well. So we can work out where the lab might have been.'

Lukas puts his head in his hands.

'I don't mind doing it on my own Lukas. If you've had enough. But Ben and the others are under too much suspicion already. If I don't try and find out a bit more about this vaccine thing, then no-one's going to do it.'

After a long silence, Lukas replies.

'I'm not letting you do this on your own,' he says, almost whispering. 'You're right Lexi. If there is even the slightest chance that we can stop any more people dying, then I'm with you.'

Chapter Twenty-Two

THE HOSPITAL

I look at Krish's map one more time.

'No. The 'Fracture Clinic' is definitely at the back of the 'Children's Ward',' I say to Lukas.

We are standing in a corridor of the hospital, tucked in a doorway, out of sight of a camera that we know is active further ahead. Krish has hacked into the hospital computer system for us so we now know all the camera protocols for the day.

Back at my house, Lukas and I had contacted him via the communication channel that Ben set up on my computer. Within an hour he had sent us the camera details and also some ancient blueprints for the hospital that he had found stored on the city council files.

'Yes, sorry,' says Lukas, turning the map around in his hands. 'I've got my right and left muddled. We need to go through this 'Children's Ward' and then through the 'Fracture Clinic' and we'll be in the 'Research' part of the hospital.'

'And which cameras will be live on that route?'

'These two. But there is a route through here. See?' Lukas says as he matches the camera locations with the map. 'And then once we are in 'Research', there's nothing.'

'I'm surprised any of them are active... since it's all closed down.'

'I guess it's just basic security.'

We wiggle our way along corridors and through empty rooms, avoiding the active cameras, until we are finally heading towards the 'Research' area. The corridor is lit with a string of artificial lights to compensate for the lack of windows and one or two of them flicker annoyingly. The walls and ceiling are painted a dull lifeless cream although occasionally someone has hung a painting on one side in an attempt to make it more homely. The floor is a bright blue with silvery speckles painted into it. I wonder if it was done to make it seem more cheerful. But since it is very worn in patches and has a sticky feel to it as I walk, it is not attractive at all. Hanging down from the ceiling at various intervals are blue and white signs. As I pass under them, I read the strange names of the departments; dermatology, radiography, geriatrics, paediatrics. All deserted now.

Finally, we are through the 'Fracture Clinic' and have passed through a set of doors marked 'Research'. It is noticeably dirtier through here and several of the ceiling lights are broken giving it a derelict feel. On either side of this corridor there are doors. We read the names of long-disappeared scientists on little metal plaques slid into holders under the frosted glass windows that sit in each one. And behind the glass, blackness; empty rooms once presumably busy with the activity of supposed alchemists.

We read the names and walk until we find it: Dr J.Z.Drachmann. On a door with ten or so others.

'Here it is Lexi,' Lukas says and he briefly holds my arm. 'Are you ready for this?'

'Yes, come on. Let's see what's still here,' I reply, pushing the door which makes a slight squeak as it opens.

The room is brighter than I expected and a glance at the ceiling reveals a row of skylights. They could do with a wash but they give enough light for us to see the room. It is big; rectangular in shape, perhaps as big as a tennis court.

Laid out in neat rows that span the full width of the room are wooden benches. They have sinks and gas taps inserted into them and under each one is a set of cupboards or drawers. On the work surfaces, there are rows of glass bottles, now covered in a thick layer of accumulated dust.

Looking up, I see that the ceiling is covered with a complex web of spring like coiled cables, wide silver foil covered tubes and all manner of other pipes. At regular intervals offshoots of these descend down in clusters to the wooden benches. I guess they supplied the workstations with air, water, gas and electricity when they were in use.

'Ethanol, Acetone, Cyclohexane,' I read from the bottles on the worktop nearest to me.

'Do you think any of this stuff is dangerous?' Lukas asks.

'I don't think it can be - if they left it here.'

Lukas walks to the edge of the room so I go to join him.

'What is that? I ask.

Ahead of us is a glass box, taller than Lukas, and on the front of it, about stomach height, are two holes. Attached to the back of the holes, currently collapsed into the box and sitting on the worktop inside, are a pair of giant green plastic gloves; big enough for someone's whole arms to fit into. Lukas puts his arms into the plastic sleeves and wiggles his fingers.

'It must protect you from whatever you're handling,' I say. 'Try and pick something up.'

On the surface inside the box, are more bottles. But there is also a syringe like object and little trays of empty glass vials. Lukas reaches for the syringe.

'You can be more precise than I would have thought,' he says and pretends to inject some liquid into the tubes.

'Look at all these computers,' I say catching sight of a bank of about thirty machines in an alcove off to the right of the lab.

'I'm not sure they're just computers,' Lukas says. 'They're all attached to big pieces of equipment. They look like some of the control screens that my dad has in his factory. You use them to tell the machines what to do.'

I lift the lid on a small box sitting on a bench. Inside it is a circular cartridge and sitting inside this are more of the small glass vials like the ones we saw in the glass case, arranged in concentric circles.

'Over here Lexi,' calls Lukas. 'There are offices.'

I rush to join him and we see that each of the researchers named outside must have had their own little office. My father's is the second one we find.

'I'm going in to see if he left any papers,' I say, opening the door. Lukas follows me.

Once inside I gaze around, imagining my barely remembered father at work in this place. I see his tall black leather chair and his desk littered with piles of papers. There are pens strewn across it and an ancient looking computer sits at one corner. Under the desk is a set of filing cabinets and another stands to one side of the room. It is to this one that I am drawn.

There are photographs on top of it; two of them. I reach to pick up the largest and run my fingers across the image of two people dressed for an old fashioned wedding ceremony. It is as if I am looking at a picture in a history book but it is my mother's face that stares back at me from beneath the white veil. I stare at the man alongside her and see my own eyes looking back at me.

'It's your mother and father?' Lukas asks.

'I guess so.'

'They looked very happy.'

'Yes, I think they were.'

I reach for the second picture and I feel the hairs on the back of my neck stand on end. I blink back my emotions and take in the image of the young man tenderly cradling a young child in his arms.

'It must be me,' I say.

'Yes,' Lukas replies quietly.

I place the photograph back and we walk over to my father's desk. For a few minutes I examine his papers.

'There's lots of stuff about chickens,' I say.

'Chickens!'

'Yes, it seems there was some worry that flu could spread from chickens to the farmers who care for them.'

'Is there anything there about the vaccine though?' Lukas asks.

'Nothing yet,' I reply.

'Well, I'm going to look back outside while you finish in here,' Lukas tells me.

And I watch him disappear back out into the laboratory.

Chapter Twenty-Three

THE THEFT

'Lexi!' Lukas shouts just a few minutes later. 'Come and look at this.'

I put down the sheaf of papers that I was flicking through and sprint outside to find him.

He is standing at the back wall of the laboratory. Lined up in front of him are about ten large metal cabinets. They look like giant fridges and each one has a circular wheel on the front of its thick door. As I arrive, he is turning one of the wheels and slowly, the door swings open. A huge plume of what looks like smoke billows out. Lukas brushes it away from his face, spluttering.

'Phwoa! It's cold,' he laughs.

Once the freezing cold air has cleared a little, I reach into the depths of the cabinet and pull one of the twenty or so drawers towards me. It is full of tiny tubes like those we've seen all over the laboratory, packed in neat rows. Lukas reaches into the drawer and removes one of them.

'What does it say on the label?' I ask.

'Influenza vaccine strain H5 N9, May 2009.'

'What does that mean?'

'I've no idea but May 2009 must have been just before your father was taken away.'

'So do you think this is the vaccine he wrote about in the article?'

'I guess it could be, couldn't it?'

I look at the tiny vial.

'Who could imagine that injecting this tiny bit of liquid into you would protect you from getting ill,' I say. 'But that's what the booklet said.'

'Amazing if it's true.'

I nod.

Lukas has stepped back and is staring at the whole array of cold stores now whilst I push back the drawer, close up the circular door and retighten the wheel.

'Hey - check this out Lexi,' he says.

'What?'

I peer at the fridges but can't see anything. They all seem identical.

'There.'

Lukas is pointing to a workbench just to the right of

the last fridge unit in the row.

'I don't see anything Lukas. What are you talking about?'

'The dust... or rather the lack of it... on the worktop.'

I step closer and put my eyes down to the level of the bench top. Lukas is right. There is an area at the front of the work surface that is completely clean.

'Do you think someone's been here?' I ask him. 'Recently?'

'I think they might have been, don't you?'

Even as he is finishing the question, I am turning the wheel on the front of the door closest to the bench. I brush aside the condensation clouds once the door is open and begin to pull out each drawer in turn, starting at the top.

Halfway down I stop.

'Look Lukas. A whole row of vials is missing.'

I count them.

'Twenty,' I say looking up at him. 'Someone has taken twenty vials out of this cooler.'

'We need to find out who's taken them,' I say once we have shut up the fridge and are walking back through the laboratory. 'Any idea how?'

'No. It's annoying because this must be one of the few places in Oxford that doesn't have cameras in it. Just when you need them.'

I stop.

'That's it Lukas.'

'It is?'

'Yes. You're right that there are no cameras in here.

But there are others still active in the building. We might still find something if we look back on their recordings.'

'But how are we going to do that?'

'Krish,' I say.

'Can he do that?'

'I don't know. But it's got to be worth a try.'

The two of us are standing just outside the door to my father's office. I give it one final glance.

'Hold on a minute. I just want to get something,' I say as I open the door.

Once inside, I walk over to the filing cabinet and pick up the photograph frame. Turning it over in my hands, I slide across the little catches that hold it together and the photograph drops from beneath the glass - the one of my father holding me in his arms. I pick it up and carefully put it in my pocket.

'OK,' I say when I get back to Lukas. 'Ready now. Let's go and contact Krish.'

Once we're out of the hospital, the two of us head straight for my house.

'Mum!' I call when I open the front door.

There is no reply.

'Good. Right. I'll get my tablet.'

Moments later, we are talking to Krish via the communication channel.

'Can you do it?' I ask him. 'Do you know how to get into the camera files?'

'I'll have a go. It depends where they've backed them up,' he replies. 'Give me a minute and I'll get back to you.'

The connection goes dead and Lukas and I are left staring at the home screen of my tablet. At the bottom of the screen I am now conscious of a flashing message icon. A picture of Tish sits next to it.

'That'll be that Chills video,' I say to Lukas. 'Want to watch it while we wait?'

'Why not?' he replies.

I open up the message and click on the crotchet icon to play the clip.

For a few seconds, there is just silent footage of the band leaping about on the benches in the Houses of Parliament. But then the music starts and Lukas almost instantly reaches into his pocket.

'Sorry Lexi,' he says. 'The noises are really bad. I'll need to wear these to watch.'

He rolls the soft earplugs between his thumb and first finger and puts them into his ears.

I give him an exaggerated thumbs-up signal and he laughs.

'I can still hear you! These just dampen down the sounds a bit so it's not so painful.'

'Sorry,' I say laughing.

But we are only half way through the clip when Krish's face appears in a small box at the bottom of the screen. I press pause on the Chills clip.

'Have you found something?' I type once I've expanded the text box to full screen.

'I think I have Lexi. I used the dates you gave me and checked the cameras near the Fracture Clinic. Anyone leaving the Research labs would have to pass that way. And sure enough, yesterday, there were two rather unexpected visitors to the hospital.'

'Who was it?' Lukas says in my ear but I am already typing the question to Krish.

'I'll send you the copy of the camera footage and you can see. It comes with a sound feed as well, and I think you should hear it.' __ _ _ _

'Thank you so much Krish. We owe you,' I type.

As soon as he is disconnected, I hear a loud 'ping'. The sound takes me instantly back to the night when Ben had first tried to contact me. The night I'd first met Lukas in fact. I think about how much I've discovered since then. And how much my life seems to have changed.

'Open it,' Lukas says. 'Quickly!'

I click.

The screen is filled with a picture of an empty corridor. For a moment I think it is a still photo but then, a movement catches my eye. Two men are walking towards the camera. One is tall and strides along, head held purposefully high. The other is smaller, chubbier and is almost running to keep up with his companion. The second man is carrying a circular box.

As they approach the camera, the microphone starts to pick up their conversation.

'I'm surprised it was all still there,' says the Pastor. 'Why didn't we destroy it all when we came to power?'

'Just an oversight I guess,' says Felix Canter. 'We just shut the place up and forgot about it.'

'And this is definitely the liquid that she was talking about?'

'Yes, she was a bit confused but I checked the paperwork. He was working on it when we had him arrested.'

'Do you think it really can stop people becoming ill?'

'I have no idea. But we have enough here for the key Party and Sacellum staff and all my family.'

'What do you want to do with the rest?'

'We need to destroy it Pastor. There's no way we can have anyone else finding out about this.'

As Felix Canter says this, the two men walk under the camera and out of sight. Within a few seconds, Krish's clip ends. Lukas and I stare at the black and white fuzz that fills my tablet screen.

'Do you think they were talking about my mother and father?'

'I don't know who else it could have been.'

'Perhaps my mother has remembered something about my dad's work after all. If she told them about the vaccine?'

'Maybe.'

'Do you think they'll really destroy the rest of the it?'

'Felix Canter sounded pretty determined, didn't he?'

'We need to talk to Ben and the others. We've got to do something to stop them. And quickly.'

'He's on a double shift at the Sacellum,' Lukas reminds me. 'Let's talk to him there.'

We find Ben sorting through the donations box at the

back of the Sacellum just as one faction is leaving and the next is arriving for prayers.

'Lukas, Lexi?' he says. 'Everything OK?'

'We need to talk to you Ben,' I say.

'Come out the back here then,' he replies and he leads us into a small anteroom at the side of the Sacellum. One other worker is just retying his sash and Ben smiles at him.

'Just arrived Brother James?'

'Yes Brother. See you later,' the man replies and walks through the doorway to go and help with the next prayer session.

'OK you two? What's the news?' says Ben, once Brother James has definitely left.

'We found my dad's laboratory Ben,' I say. 'It was amazing.'

'And was there anything still in it?'

'His papers were still on his desk,' I reply. 'It looked like he'd just popped out for coffee.'

'But we aren't the only ones who went there,' adds Lukas. 'The Pastor and Felix Canter were there yesterday Ben.'

'But, the Pastor was supposed to be in London,' says Ben.

'Well, he wasn't,' I reply. 'They went looking for something in my father's laboratory and they found it.'

'What was it?'

'Vaccine,' says Lukas.

'The stuff you told me about Lexi - that stopped people getting sick?'

I nod.

'There were thousands of little tiny glass vials in huge fridges,' Lukas says. 'And they took some of it.'

'To use?'

'They said so.'

'And they also said they were going to destroy the rest,' I add.

Ben thinks for few moments.

'And you really think this liquid can stop people getting sick Lexi.'

'I just don't know Ben. It's what my father was working on... and something my mother has said has clearly made the Pastor believe it is possible.'

'And there is lots left?'

'Yes,' says Lukas 'There's enough there to treat thousands of people.'

'Then we have to work out a way of doing just that,' says Ben.

Chapter Twenty-Four

THE DOWNFALL

'Alexa Drachmann?' asks the man in front of me when I open our front door three hours later.

'Yes,' I manage to reply squeakily as I stare in panic at his yellow cloak.

'The Pastor would like to see you in the Sacellum... now.'

I vaguely nod my head and automatically turn to reach for my own, white, shroud. It briefly occurs to me that I should leave a note for my mother. But as soon as the hood is pulled tight over my head, the Enforcer takes me by the elbow and pulls me out of the front door. This one simple action is enough. I stare at the clawed hand gripping my silk covered arm, and I make a decision.

'I can walk perfectly well by myself,' I say and wrench myself away from him. I step quickly outside and stare directly into the lens of the camera that I see tracking my every move. I am going to make this journey on my own terms, so I take him by surprise and stride up the road towards the Sacellum.

Step after step I am aware of increasing numbers of people staring at me; coming to their doorsteps, stopping their street-side conversations, all silenced by the sight of my detention. I hear my name whispered around me, then my mother's name. But it just makes me more determined that they will not intimidate me. I will face whatever they are going to throw at me with as much courage as I can muster.

When we arrive at the Sacellum, I see that word has got out about some trouble and there is a small crowd already gathering. Inside, I can hear a prayer session is still in progress but the Enforcer doesn't stop and although I have paused by the front door, he pushes me roughly inside.

I walk into the cold, dark building and the assembled congregation falls silent. For once, the Pastor is leading the prayers in person. Arriving at the centre aisle, I stop and look him straight in the eyes. I catch a supercilious lopsided smile flit across his face. I know I should walk towards him, start apologising for whatever I think I have done wrong.

But I don't move. I don't open my mouth and I don't walk. Seconds pass and he is soon getting visibly annoyed. After a minute, I hear someone whisper to me.

'Walk girl! Don't be stupid.'

But I stand firm.

And then I hear a commotion at the doorway; there are voices outside and suddenly, the door is thrown open a second time. An overweight Enforcer enters, pushing someone roughly in front of him. I can't see who it is; they are just an outline against the sunshine.

'Get in there you ungrateful sinner,' shouts the huge man in yellow and he shoves his captive towards me. The figure stumbles across the flagstones and I am aware of the colour of the cloak enveloping their body. I feel nausea rise in my throat.

It is red.

Lukas lifts his head and I see he has been treated far worse than I have. Blood streams down his chin and one arm hangs by his side whilst he supports his body against the pillars that line the aisle.

Before I can reach out to him, I catch the look of warning in his eyes.

'Well, well, well,' comes the Pastor's voice from behind me. 'So now we have both of our guilty children with us.'

I turn back to face him and feel the anger rising in my chest once more; the vicious bully is enjoying himself.

'Come now, Lukas and Alexa... come and join me here at the Altar.'

I still do not move and Lukas rests against the pillar, equally reluctant to approach the figure standing with his arms spread out wide as if welcoming guests into his home.

'I said come and join me,' he repeats, more sternly now.

Lukas moves first. Just a little initially, but I guess he's decided that he will face the Pastor. As he draws level with me, I move to walk beside him up the aisle. We don't say a word and we don't look at one another.

The congregation is starting to mutter, asking one another what we have done. This appears to agitate the Pastor and so, before we even arrive in front of him, he begins to list our supposed crimes.

'Look in shame upon these two young people,' he begins. 'For they have broken some of our most precious and sacred rules.'

I am waiting to hear what we are accused of with as much anticipation as everyone else now. A black robed figure steps forward and hands the Pastor a brown folder and he ceremoniously opens it and starts to hold up a series of images.

'Our loyal team of Enforcers have recorded them on numerous occasions,' he continues, waving the photographs over his head theatrically. 'And as you can see... '

But the Pastor is interrupted by a burst from the Sacellum whistle. Turning around to see what is happening, I see the crowds at the back of the building begin to part. At first all I can distinguish is a black robed figure, his white sash swaying wildly as he almost sprints down the centre aisle. But as he approaches I see that it is Ben. Is he to be accused alongside us?

But then I notice that Ben is unaccompanied. Or at least, he is not with an Enforcer. He is, in fact, being followed by the tall figure of Felix Canter.

'Pastor,' Felix Canter shouts as he strides towards the three of us at the Altar. 'Please halt these proceedings immediately.'

'I'm sorry sir,' the Pastor stutters. 'I... don't understand sir... '

'I ordered you to stop immediately. There has been a mistake.'

'I assure you not sir,' the Pastor continues and he picks up his folder of photographs and thrusts it towards the Party leader. 'Take a look for yourself, sir.'

'There is no need for that,' says Felix Canter. 'I know these two young people well.'

'But... '

'There is no need to concern yourself further Pastor. I am well aware that these two have been spending time together. Lukas is allocated to my daughter and Alexa is her best friend. They had every reason to be together.'

'But still... '

'I instructed you to leave them alone Pastor. I am making that a Party Order. Are you disobeying me?'

'No... no,' the Pastor says, his voice barely above a whisper. 'I thought you would appreciate my looking after your daughter's wellb... '

'Good,' interrupts Felix Canter. 'Then they can go. Yes?'

'Ye-es,' the Pastor whispers reluctantly.

Felix Canter turns to us and shoos us away like a pair of buzzing flies. I stare at him but, unusually, he avoids making any eye contact. Instead he turns straight back to the Pastor.

'I need a private word with you.'

'You do?' asks the Pastor.

I can see from his expression that confusion has now morphed into fear and only slowly does he follow Felix Canter towards his private rooms at the back of the Sacellum. Watching them walk away, I am suddenly aware that everyone else is silently staring at Lukas and me again.

'There is nothing happening here,' comes Ben's voice. 'Please consider this the end of the service and continue with your daily routine ladies and gentlemen.'

His words seem to break the spell and everyone begins to talk at once. They leave the Sacellum, gathering in little huddles to discuss the events, occasionally looking back over their shoulders at us.

'Are you OK Lukas?' Ben asks once the crowds nearest to us have moved away.

'I think my arm is broken,' he replies.

'Lexi?'

'Yeh... fine... ' is all I can muster.

'Come on then. Let's get out of here,' Ben says. 'You need to get home Lexi. I told your mother to wait there. And I need to take Lukas to a nurse.'

'But Ben... ' I say.

'Yes?'

'What just happened?'

'What do you mean?'

'Why was Felix Canter here? And why did he stop the Pastor?'

'Let's walk,' is his only reply.

Dazed, we follow his instructions. Several people are still outside, but the presence of Ben escorting us seems to make them satisfied that we have, after all, been forgiven by the authorities.

'So go on Ben,' I say as we walk towards my road. 'Are you going to explain?'

'I just thought we should involve Felix Canter in the decision as to what should happen to you.'

'You knew that the Pastor was after us?' I say. 'That we were in trouble?'

'I heard an hour ago. Just after you left me.'

'What was he going to do to us?'

'Does it matter?' he replies. 'Suffice it to say, it was serious enough for me to know I had to do something.'

'What was in that file?'

'Just pictures,' Ben says. '... but alot of them. You've not been very careful you two. And the Enforcers are pretty good at spotting patterns.'

'What do you mean?' Lukas asks.

'Oh you know, the same two people appearing together too often in the same places.'

'But most of the cameras have been red recently... '

'Yes, it would appear that there has been some local assistance too. One of your neighbours Lexi, who became suspicious.'

I think about this briefly, but there is no point in trying to work out who it might have been. Lukas and I have been together a lot. There is no denying that, so it could have been several people.

'But why did you think Felix Canter would help us Ben?' I ask.

'I suppose I hoped he would have no choice,' Ben replies.

'What do you mean?' Lukas asks him.

'I... er... told him we knew he had given vaccinations to all his family.'

I stop. I turn to look at Ben.

'You did what!' I shout.

'Shhh, Lexi. Keep your voice down,' he replies. 'There's only so much trouble I can get you out of in one day.'

'But Ben. You TOLD him?'

'Yes.'

'But how did you say you knew?' asks Lukas.

'I didn't.'

'And he didn't try to deny it?' I ask.

'Of course he did, but I took a guess and told him we could prove it from the mark on his arm. That's where you said he'd have injected it - right Lexi?'

'Yes, but... '

'I told him we'd brand him as an alchemist,' Ben continues.

'And what did he say?'

'Well, he tried to deny all knowledge at first, but when I said we'd involve Laetitia, he caved in as fast as anything.'

I stand for a minute, absorbing this news.

'But then what did you say to him?' I ask.

'I just suggested he needed to get you out of trouble or people would find out what he had done.'

'And that was it?'

'Yes,' Ben adds. 'I did suggest he might need to work out a way of discrediting the Pastor in order to really remove the suspicion from the two of you... '

'Discrediting the Pastor?'

'Yes, you know. So people would think he was making you two seem like sinners to cover for himself.'

'Ben!' I say. 'I can't believe this. Didn't you think he might just have you locked up?'

'I wondered. But luckily I think he was worried that there might be other people who knew about the vaccinations, so he decided to go with my plan.'

We have reached my house now and as we approach the driveway the front door is flung open and my mother races out.

'Lexi!' she shouts. She hugs me briefly and turns to Ben. 'Thankyou Brother. Thankyou so much for whatever you said.'

'You're welcome Mrs. Drachmann,' Ben says. 'It was all a misunderstanding. But Mr. Canter has cleared it up so please don't worry.'

'Mr. Canter?' she replies.

'Yes, but as I say, it is all sorted out now.'

My mother and I stand and watch Ben and Lukas walk towards the nurse's surgery and then we turn to walk inside. I know I will have lots of questions to answer from her but that doesn't bother me. I am much more worried about Felix Canter. After the shock of the detention and the drama of events in the Sacellum, I am now left with the uncomfortable feeling that Felix Canter and I have some unfinished business.

Chapter Twenty-Five

THE DEAL

Lying on my bed listening to some music, I'm feeling calmer that I've done for weeks. I've forgotten how much better it makes me feel about things and for a few moments I can almost remember how life felt before this terrible sickness arrived. I know that the sun is shining outside and I can vaguely hear a few birds singing.

But then it all floods back.

Although I try to concentrate on the peacefulness of the morning, all I can think about is the message last night on the Flow; Harriet James and Sophie Hodgkins from my class at school are dead. We knew they were ill, but the rumour had been that they were getting better. And the worst thing is that we won't even be allowed to mention their names in class because they were sinners. Mrs Evers, our headmistress, has made that very plain to us in her daily announcements.

I'm just remembering the way that Harriet used to make us all laugh with her wicked impressions of various teachers, when I hear a low purring hum in the road outside. Getting up to look out of my window, I see Felix Canter's black limousine glide to a stop outside our front gate. I watch as his peaked-capped chauffeur gets out and makes his way down the path to our front door. The doorbell rings.

I take three deep breaths, look around my bedroom and go to my door. Slowly, I descend the stairs.

'Lex... '

My mother stops when she sees me and walks forwards. We have been expecting this and we are prepared. Over the last three days, we have talked and talked. I have told her everything that Lukas and I have discovered and she has told me everything that she can remember about the time before the Collapse, about my father and about her life. Neither of us have dared to think too hard about Felix Canter's next move but we knew that it would come before too long.

'Mr. Canter requests your company,' says the chauffeur politely.

'Of course,' I reply.

I take my robe. I let my mother help me adjust it correctly. We both need this moment to pass without tension. I hug her.

'I love you,' she whispers.

'You too,' I reply.

When we arrive at the Lodge in Dartford College, Peters is already manning the door and I am instantly swept through the front hallway towards Felix Canter's study. More than anything, I had hoped to be spared the sight of Tish watching me arrive and it seems Felix Canter has at least allowed me - or perhaps his daughter - this one concession. Walking towards the heavy oak door, I remember the day when I stole into the study with Lukas. I knew then that Felix Canter was not someone to be toyed with. And part of me wishes that I had remembered that along the way. But only part of me.

'Come in,' comes his deep voice when Peters knocks.

'Miss Alexa Drachmann sir.'

I enter and Felix Canter rises from his desk. For a moment we face each other silently, but then he speaks.

'Please come and take a seat.'

I walk over to one of the chairs near the window and sit down. As I sink into the soft cushion, I notice the stone folly in the garden - with its carved bust. Quickly I turn back to look at Tish's father lowering himself slowly into the deep leather chair opposite me.

'Gladstone... ' he says. '... but of course, you know that, don't you?'

I nod.

'Very resourceful of you.'

I don't reply.

'Resourceful, but stupid. I warned you to stay out of things you don't understand Alexa.'

I ram my hands under my knees to stop them shaking.

'And I suspect that you have not heeded my warning.'

I still remain mute.

At this point, Felix Canter suddenly rises from the chair, and it makes me flinch. He stands, towering over me, for a few seconds but then turns and reaches for something on his desk; a brown file.

'You have to help the people who aren't sick yet,' I say finally, with as much strength in my voice as I can muster.

My mother and I have agreed that I have one chance to try to help people and that I should use it. If I'm going to be sent for realignment, I may as well try to help everyone else first.

'You want to talk about the sick?' he says, looking surprised.

'Yes. You have to give them the vaccine,' I say.

'I see. So you know about the vaccine.'

'I know about it and I believe it will save people.'

'And if I refuse?'

'Then hundreds more will die. And the sickness will spread across the country.'

'But why should I help them? Reveal to them that the work of an alchemist can save them when prayer has not.'

'Because it is the truth.'

He throws back his head and laughs.

'The truth!'

'Yes. And you are willing to use it to save your own family.'

Felix Canter briefly looks wrong footed.

'I will deny it,' he mutters.

I pause and decide it is time to play my only strong card.

'I have a recording of you... at the hospital with the Pastor... taking the vaccine for yourself.'

Once more he looks uncertain but quickly composes himself.

'So it was you that told Brother Benedict?' he says.

'Yes.'

'I wondered,' he says, almost smiling to himself. 'But no matter. I'll simply have him removed and you sent away for realignment.'

'Why didn't you just let the Pastor punish me then?' I retort.

'And have my daughter's best friend exposed in public as a Blasphemer?' he asks, looking more angry again now. 'Much better to deal with you in private.'

'You can do what you like to me,' I reply, getting to my feet now. 'Other people know what you did; not just me and Ben.'

'Ah yes... and by that I presume you mean Lukas Svoboda,' he says, pushing me back into my seat with a firm shove to my chest. 'My intended son in law.'

I stare up at him, temporarily thrown; I had meant Carrie, Josh and Krish. It hadn't occurred to me that he would involve Lukas. As I absorb his words, Felix Canter throws the brown file onto my lap. It is the one that I had last seen in the Pastor's hands in the Sacellum.

'You might want to explain these to me Alexa,' he says. 'Do you think my daughter, your best friend, would like to see these shots of you with her future husband.'

'He's just my friend,' I reply. 'I love Tish. I would never hurt her.'

'But these photographs *would* hurt her.'

I flick through them. I am astonished by how many there are. Some taken in the street, some near my house and then others down on Portmeadow. At the back of the file I see two from the hospital and it occurs to me that perhaps the cameras are live more often than they appear.

'They are misleading,' I say. 'They are just pictures of two people talking or paying respects at someone's grave.'

'Are they Alexa?'

'Yes,' I say, fixing him firmly in the eye. 'They are.'

'And Lukas... how does he feel about you Alexa? Have you asked yourself that?'

'He doesn't feel anything for me,' I say dismissively.

'No?'

'We are just friends,' I repeat.

'Well, you cannot be friends in this society. You know that.'

'I know it,' I mutter. 'But I don't understand it.'

He reaches over and takes back the file of photographs.

'I chose that boy for my daughter. He is kind, respectful and intelligent. His family are devout and loyal to the Party. I wasn't going to let her be allocated to some arrogant fool desperate for influence and political power. And I will not allow you to come between them.'

I'm surprised by this; that Tish's father might actually

have been behind their allocation. That he might have specifically chosen Lukas.

'We have just been trying to answer some questions Mr. Canter,' I say to try and get him back onto the issue of the vaccine. 'We didn't set out to hurt anyone. We just didn't understand what was going on.'

'But people are going to get hurt Alexa.'

'And people will die if you do nothing.'

'They will go to meet their Creator and live in happiness in his kingdom.'

'It will come out that you could have saved them. Eventually it will.'

Felix Canter suddenly walks over to the Leonardo da Vinci painting on the wall. He studies it for a moment and then turns back to me. My heart is thudding like a base-drum in my chest.

'So you want me to find a way to give everyone this vaccine then?'

'I do,' I say uncertainly, waiting for the trap to be sprung.

For five seconds, maybe ten, silence fills the space between us.

'Alright, so this will be our deal then... you and I... '

He steps forward and leans over me; so close to me that I can feel his breath on my face. I do my best to keep eye contact.

'I will find a way to provide the vaccine for the community... '

Relief floods over me.

'... and you will stay away from Lukas Svoboda. You will leave my daughter to be happy with the boy I chose for her.'

I wait to hear more but that is it. No realignment. No detention. Just another deal. Like those that my mother and father made before me. The community gets treatment and I have to agree not to see Lukas. Easy.

As I peer into his flinty eyes, I suddenly comprehend that this has been about Tish all along. He risked everything he believes in to save her with that vaccine. He could never have allowed me to be harmed by the Pastor because she wouldn't forgive him for that. And now he must ensure she gets the husband he wants for her.

And of course I do not wish to hurt Tish either. I can barely believe how straightforward this has turned out to be.

'Yes,' I say. 'It's a deal.'

I walk through the door that Felix Canter holds open for me and cross the polished wooden floor. I am almost in the front hallway, when I hear Tish's voice coming from the sitting room and she emerges into the hallway with Lukas.

'Lexi!' she screams and runs towards me. 'What are you doing here?'

I look over her shoulder and see Felix Canter watching me.

'I just needed to see your father about something,' I reply.

'Daddy?' she replies. 'What did you need to see him about?'

She appears perplexed but her father is instantly

prepared.

'We were just discussing some details about your allocation ceremony. I thought your oldest friend might have some inside knowledge.'

I see her face light up with delight.

'Did you tell him about the dress?' she whispers in my ear.

I nod and Tish giggles.

'Can you stay a bit Lexi?' she asks. 'Lukas is just going. He has to get his arm checked out.'

I have been studiously ignoring him but I do turn briefly to glance in Lukas' direction now, and see that his arm is encased in plaster right up over the elbow.

'Did you hear what that enforcer did to him?' Tish asks.

'I did,' I reply.

'It's fine,' says Lukas, sounding embarrassed. 'Just a misunderstanding.'

'I still think Daddy should have him punished,' says Tish.

'It's all sorted out Laetitia,' Felix Canter says firmly, but as I watch him placate his daughter, I notice that he isn't actually looking at her.

He is looking over her shoulder - at Lukas.

When I turn my attention back to Lukas to see why, I discover that he is staring straight at me.

And there is such an intense look of concern on his face that I have to turn away.

'I need to go now Tish,' I say rapidly. 'Sorry. I have to go and help mum with... something. I'll come over later though.'

Without waiting for a reply, I storm through the front door and out into the street as quickly as I can.

For I now know that Felix Canter was correct. Lukas Svoboda would indeed appear to feel far more for me that I had realised.

Chapter Twenty-Six

THE END

The people are queuing all along the pathway that leads to the Sacellum. When I arrive, I take my place and wait to hear my name. People leaving are rubbing their arms and there is a general hum of conversation about this miraculous liquid that they have been told will give them the Creator's protection from the sickness.

'Remember, you must fully reveal the true nature of your sins to the Creator,' says the Sacellum worker as a young woman kneels to pray. 'He will know if you are not repentant and the elixir will have no protective effect.'

The Sacellum has been offering the vaccinations for

over a week now. The factions have been treated one by one and I am relieved that my own turn has finally come. Already though, my mother says there are fewer people coming to her nursing centres. It seems that this illness is the one that my father and his colleagues had been dreading for so long; the one that the vaccination was designed for.

'Alexa Drachmann.'

I step forward and kneel, looking up at the portrait of Nathaniel Jefferies. This particular one shows his head and shoulders. I carefully examine the face that I have superficially observed every day for most of my life; the immaculately styled grey hair, tanned face and piercing blue eyes. I wonder what he knew about Charles Darwin and everything that I learned about in the caverns under the Bodleian. A sudden burst of bird song outside punctures the air and I remember Darwin's finches.

'Lexi,' comes a whisper to my right and I see Ben in the shadows. I get up and make my way across to talk to him. But as I do so, something suddenly slots into place in my head.

'Ben!'

'Yes?'

'Birds!'

'What?'

'If this illness is avian flu like my dad thought,' I say. 'Then I think that means we got it from birds.'

'You do?'

'Yes. Avis... it's Latin for birds,' I say. 'Avian flu must be a flu from birds.'

I look back at the portrait. Something about it... the

eyes...

'Majorelle Blue,' I say quietly.

'What?' asks Ben, sounding confused.

'The parrots.'

'What? Lexi, are you ill?'

I laugh.

'No Ben, don't panic. I just think I might have worked out what's been going on for the last few weeks.'

'You have?'

'Yes, I think someone needs to go and tell Mr. Mansour to get rid of his parrots!'

'What? Why?'

I stop for a moment to gather my thoughts.

'My dad... he knew that a bird flu would one day infect humans... an avian flu... and that was what he and the other researchers prepared for. They thought it would come from chickens.'

'OK... '

'But I just realised. Mr. Mansour's niece was one of the first people to become ill.'

'Yes?'

'And they had just bought those parrots for their shop.'

'You think the illness came from the parrots.'

'It could have done, couldn't it?'

'I guess so.'

'We should tell someone.'

'I will,' says Ben. 'As soon as I'm off-duty later.'

We stand together at the side of the Sacellum and I can tell Ben is still thinking about what I've just said. I watch him and recall his coming to my house only a few weeks ago and causing me such a panic when he asked me to go with him. I smile to myself and then suddenly notice his sash; it has an extra gold stripe stitched on it.

'Hey - you've been promoted!'

'Yes, apparently it was on Felix Canter's orders.'

I raise my eyebrows.

'So what does it mean?'

'I'm effectively second in command. To be honest, I was running the place when the Pastor was avoiding doing prayer sessions, but at least it's official now.'

'Congratulations Ben.'

'Thanks. I hope the new Pastor turns out to be better than the last.'

'Is it true what they say then? That the old one is gone for good.'

'Gone and in real trouble apparently.'

'Really?'

'Yes, Felix Canter stitched him up. He told the authorities that the Pastor had just vaccinated himself when he got hold of the elixir.'

'And they believed him?'

'They checked the Pastor's arm.'

'And not Mr. Canter's?'

'No - luckily for him. He made it seem as if the Pastor was going to keep the elixir for himself,' says Ben. 'And then made himself a hero by announcing it would be used to save anyone who would fully repent their sins.'

'Did the Pastor not try to embroil Mr. Canter?'

'I think he tried. But who would believe such an important Party official would be involved?'

'Wow. The perks of political power,' I say.

'But anyway, the most important thing is that people are getting treated. Well done Lexi.'

'Me?'

'Yes, you understood what the vaccine could do.'

'It was my father's work.'

'But you made Felix Canter use it.'

'Not just me Ben... others too. You in particular.'

'Perhaps... '

'I wouldn't have been involved at all if you hadn't started to notice that the facts were changing on the Flow.'

'Maybe. Which reminds me... Carrie was released!'

'Yes! When?'

'Last night. Josh is over the moon.'

'I bet he is. Is she OK?'

He nods.

'She's lost lots of weight and I wouldn't exactly say that their attempts to realign her have been very successful but she's OK and she's free.'

'That's fantastic Ben.'

'Perhaps when things have settled down a bit you'll come over and we'll get everyone together again.'

'Really... do you want to keep meeting?'

'Of course. Nothing's changed. In fact, things have only got more strange. And we need to get those papers out of your house.'

'I guess, but won't we be being watched.'

'I'm not sure. But we do need to decide what to do next with what we know. I was wondering if we should find a way to contact someone in Scientia... see if they are interested in what you found down in the Bodleian... or what we've worked out about the disruption of people's memories.'

I stare at him.

'That sounds risky. Are you sure?'

'There are still too many unanswered questions Lexi.'

'I suppose so... '

'Will you tell Lukas?'

I pause and study my shoes.

'What is it?'

'Nothing. I just don't think Lukas will be able to come any more.'

Ben lifts my chin gently with his hand.

'Why? What's happened?'

'Nothing. I... '

'Yes?'

'I... just can't see him anymore.'

'But you two seemed to get on so well.'

'Yes... I suppose we did... but I've made a promise to someone. I can't say anymore Ben. Don't ask me.'

He looks at me uncertainly.

'That's a shame,' he says quietly.

I turn away.

'It's fine. I need to get my vaccination,' I say quickly and I cross the Sacellum to join the queue to see the nurse.

An hour later and I'm walking along my road, protected from the sickness. The throbbing in my arm reminds me of my father and I wonder if my mother is right; she is sure he is still safe somewhere, thinking of us.

I have put the photo of him holding me as a baby in the drawer of my bedside table. Every night before I go to sleep, I wish him a safe night, wherever he is spending it. I hope he would be proud that his work is saving so many people. If I'm right, then Mr. Mansour had no idea that his beautiful blue parrots could make everyone so sick. But my father always understood that one day a deadly bird flu would be able to infect humans and then be passed from one person to another.

Once I'm home, I hang up my robe and go to my room. I lie back on the bed and look up at my posters.

'Of course - Xentricity! I should've guessed,' says Lukas' voice in my head.

I almost laugh at the memory and am just thinking that I should tell him my idea about the parrots, when I remember.

That I can't.

And an increasingly familiar sinking feeling flutters in my stomach.

When I was sitting in Felix Canter's study a week ago it seemed so easy to agree to his deal. And, when I saw Lukas' face as I left, I just felt stupid for not having realised how he felt about me.

But since then, something has changed. Despite what I said to Ben, the truth is that I have really missed Lukas.

And this fills me with fear – because I really can't allow myself to care about him at all.

THE END

Coming Soon...

THE SCIENTIA

Chapter One

THE ESCAPE

Walking into the kitchen I see an envelope sitting propped up against a mug of cold tea. A note from my mother sits beside it on a small pad.

> 'See you later Lexi
> I've gone down to open up the stall.
> Make sure you eat some breakfast when you eventually get out of bed.
> A messenger brought this for you earlier, Mum x'

I throw the tea down the sink and pour a glass of orange juice instead. Once I'm sat at the kitchen table, I reach for the envelope and tear it open. Removing the card causes a flurry of tiny glittering paper horseshoes to tumble onto the table in front of me. I turn over the square of cream parchment and read the first few words printed on it.

'Please join us to celebrate the union of our daughter Laetitia to Mr. Lukas Svoboda... '

I drop the card. A bubble of emotion seems to swell deep inside me. I can't move, I just stare at the words confirming the date and time of the ceremony - at least a year before it needed to be - but still three months away.

The initial shock having passed, I tidy away the invitation and the mess of decorations from the envelope. I reach for my tablet and call up my home page to find something to distract me. Several icons are flashing, but my eyes are drawn to the live news feed banner that is moving across the bottom of the screen.

'… Breaking News: Department for Realignment confirms that ten alchemists have broken out of a facility near Henley on Thames… '

With a series of flicks of my wrist, I locate the News Channel and watch the newsreader as he gives an update on the situation.

'… A spokesman says that the ten are considered to be no danger to public but that any information as to their whereabouts should be provided as soon as possible to any local Enforcer. These particular individuals are reputed to have proved almost impossible to rehabilitate. They include star gazers, Jacob Jones and William Renney and the experimental alchemist J.Z. Drachmann… '

I stare at the name. J. Z. Drachmann. My father.

And then I hear the telltale 'ping' of a message arriving in my inbox. I tap distractedly on the image of the post box that sits in the corner of the screen. The new message explodes in front of my eyes.

'I need to see you. I miss you. Lukas.'

… to be continued

ACKNOWLEDGEMENTS

One reason I wrote this book was to encourage young people – especially young girls – to be interested in science and how it can improve our lives. So in the most general sense, I must first thank all the inspirational science teachers that taught me over the years, at school and university. You really did leave me with a lifelong passion for the subject.

In terms of getting the book written, I am grateful to my whole extended family for their support. But to my parents, Richard and Dot Owen, I must say a particular thank you; for always encouraging my love of science and latterly, the crazy idea that I could write a novel incorporating it!

My fantastic friends deserve a mention. You cannot know how uplifting it was to have my idea greeted with such excitement and how much your interest has meant to me. Amongst the group, special thanks must go to Sarah Boden, Dom Winks, Ilja Holland-Kaye, Sophia Krakowian, Emma Wilson, Jackie King-Turner, Helen Tapper, Selina Porter and Clare Martin.

Thank you to Anna-Beth Brogan for being the first impartial guinea pig reader of The Flow and to Shelley Instone who edited it for me and taught me so much about writing for children.

But of course, the biggest cheer must go to my lovely husband and two wonderful children: for keeping me going with ideas, constructive criticism, and most importantly, a sense of humour.

ABOUT THE AUTHOR

Caroline Martin read Natural Sciences at Cambridge University and Epidemiology at The London School of Hygiene and Tropical Medicine. She has also worked in Corporate Strategy and Acquisitions but decided that she found science far more interesting.

She lives in Oxford with her husband, two children and a cat called Rosie who keeps her lap warm whilst she writes.